"I'm not afraid of you,"
Gloryanne said.

As if to prove it, she stared defiantly up into Logan's hard, handsome face.

"You ought to be," he said silkily.

His eyes slid over her, and his expression was so dismissive it made her feel suddenly reckless. "You know what your problem is, Bradshaw?"

"What?"

"You've spent too much time around kids and horses who have to do what you say because you're the boss. But you're not *my* boss—so why don't you take a hike?" Planting her hands on his chest, she gave him a shove. It wasn't strong enough to actually move him, but it did manage to rock him back on his heels.

His hands shot out and encircled her wrists. "The only thing I'm going to take," he growled, "is this." Then he hauled her into his arms, and his mouth came down to smother her protests....

MARRY ME,
Cowboy

DANGEROUS
Caroline Cross

Silhouette Books

Published by Silhouette Books
America's Publisher of Contemporary Romance

SILHOUETTE BOOKS

ISBN 0-373-65315-8

DANGEROUS

Copyright © 1993 by Jen M. Heaton

First Silhouette Books printing September 1993

Visit Silhouette at www.eHarlequin.com

Printed in U.S.A.

CAROLINE CROSS

always loved to read, but it wasn't until she discovered romance that she felt compelled to write, fascinated by the chance to explore the positive power of love in people's lives. She grew up in Yakima, Washington, the "Apple Capital of the World," attended the University of Puget Sound and now lives outside Seattle, where she *tries to* work at home despite the chaos created by two telephone-addicted teenage daughters and a husband with a fondness for home-improvement projects. Pleased to have recently been #1 on a national bestseller list, she was thrilled to win the 1999 Romance Writers of America RITA® Award for Best Short Contemporary Novel and to have been called "one of the best" writers of romance today by *Romantic Times* magazine. Caroline believes in writing from the heart—and having a good brainstorming partner. She loves hearing from readers and can be reached at P.O. Box 47375, Seattle, Washington 98146. Please include a SASE for reply.

To Peggy Riecan for always being there for me,
and to Sandy Kujath for her encouragement
and thoughtful critiques

One

Dangerous. The word came to Gloryanne Rossiter's mind the instant she saw him standing in the shadow of the horse barn.

He was cloaked in darkness, his features obscured. Yet she could feel the weight of his gaze as it played across her suddenly sensitive skin—and she knew, as she peered through the dusty windshield of her red Jeep Cherokee, that he was watching her, too.

To the east, dawn was breaking, the rising sun sending brilliant fingers of orange, gold and scarlet shooting across the stark Columbia River landscape. A lone whippoorwill sang a bittersweet song, the sound floating on the bright fall air which was fragrant with the scent of sage.

And still Gloryanne couldn't tear her gaze from the man. She chided herself for being foolish. Yet, even as she attributed her sudden flight of fancy to tiredness—the drive from southwestern Oregon to this small ranch in central Washington had been a grueling one—she couldn't deny her uneasiness. Nor her sudden certainty that he wasn't about to welcome her warmly to this place where she hoped to make a new start.

She had every right to be here, she reminded herself. Unlike the situation with Jack Waylan, her former employer and ex-fiancé, she no longer had to prove what an asset she could be. She *owned* part of this place, and nothing—and no one—could take that away.

The thought was bracing. She got out of the Cherokee, shut the door with a decisive bang and started across the stable yard. "Good morning," she called, temporarily blinded as she stepped from the bright sunlight into the shade cast by the barn. "I'm Gloryanne Rossiter, Melanie's cousin."

For a moment there was silence. And then came a voice as dark as a moonless night. "Ms. Rossiter." The man seemed to materialize out of the gloom, gathering substance as he came closer to the light. "Logan Bradshaw."

He inclined his head and she rocked to a halt, her eyes widening as she got her first clear look at him standing there with his long legs braced apart and his lean, muscled arms crossed. The pose stretched an ancient denim jacket across his broad shoulders, the pale blue fabric enhancing his dark glossy hair, navy eyes and strongly chiseled features the way a custom frame sets off an original painting.

Dangerous, Glory thought again, feeling a momentary pang in the face of his startling male beauty. She gave herself a shake. Jack had been nice-looking, too, she reminded herself dryly, and look what that had gotten her—unemployment and homelessness at the age of twenty-six.

"I thought I made it clear when you called that this wasn't a good time for a visit." Logan Bradshaw interrupted her musing with exaggerated politeness.

Gloryanne stiffened. "As a matter of fact, you did." Even though she preferred his bluntness to the web of misconceptions she'd been tangled in for the past six months, his antagonism rankled. "But as I explained, this isn't a visit, and I don't need either your approval or your permission to be here, Mr. Bradshaw. According to the attorney handling my cousin's estate, Melanie was perfectly within her rights to leave me the share of the ranch she received when the two of you divorced. Just as *I'm* perfectly within my rights to take up residence here." Despite the inflammatory nature of the words, Glory's tone was mild. She intended, after all, to live with this man—in a manner of speaking.

"Yeah," he said. Although his aloof expression never changed, the deep blue of his eyes intensified before his gaze dropped to study the square toe of one well-worn cowboy boot. "Legally, I suppose you are."

For a moment Gloryanne was fooled by his smooth voice into thinking the matter settled. Then, when he raised his head and she saw the nerve ticking in his jaw and the turbulent emotion swirling in his midnight eyes, she knew that she was wrong.

His incredible blue gaze seared her like a laser beam. "Except that I don't want you here, Ms. Rossiter," he said with finality. "I told you that. This is a conservative community, and I've got no housekeeper and two kids to raise. You can't just sashay in here like you own the place.'' Low and husky, his voice reflected his growing frustration, as did the impatient way he ran a hand through his thick, shining hair. He glowered at her.

Glory didn't so much as flinch, returning his intent stare with what she hoped was credible calm. But inside she wavered. It wasn't her intention to disrupt Logan Bradshaw's life; she was only trying to salvage her own.

Her chin rose slightly. "I'm sorry you're uncomfortable with my decision to come here, but I *do* own the place. At least," she amended, "a third of it. And I find it hard to believe your neighbors are going to condemn you because one of your son's relatives has come to stay.'' When the news had come that Melanie had died in a car accident, unexpectedly leaving her share of her ex-husband's horse ranch to Glory, Glory had been stunned. It had been inexplicable that a woman she'd hardly known would leave her such a bequest—but so wonderful.

She needed Columbia Creek, and the time it would take to heal the wounds Jack had inflicted to her self-respect. But more than that, she *wanted* it. For so long she'd been hungry for a place to call home. Now she had it, and she couldn't—she wouldn't—turn her back and walk away, no matter Logan Bradshaw's enmity.

Remembering the miles of apple orchard she'd driven through on her way in, she slowly surveyed the big, weathered barn, the indoor arena and the dozen or so sleek, well-fed horses occupying a chain of corrals. Her gaze came back to him, her whiskey-colored eyes probing his blue ones intently. "What about the rest of your help? Surely one of them lives in and can fill the role of chaperon?''

His expression grew even more shuttered. ''Melanie's hotshot lawyer must've told you that the orchards are leased. And as for the rest of it... Well, not that it's any of your business, but Seth, my foreman, is staying with his sister while he recovers from a broken leg, and there's nobody else I'd consider. Besides,'' he went briskly on, ''I think if you take a good look around, you'll realize this ranch isn't right for you.''

He gestured at the hills, dun-colored after the summer heat except where row after row of irrigated apple trees marched in symmetrical, dark green formation. ''This is the boonies, Ms. Rossiter. We're on the Columbia, smack in the middle of nowhere. Seattle's a hundred and fifty miles thataway.'' He pointed roughly northwest. ''And Spokane's just as far away over there.'' He gestured northeast.

''Nile, of course,'' his handsome face mirrored the sudden mockery in his tone, ''is only twelve miles north, but I sincerely doubt it's what you're accustomed to. In case you blinked when you drove through, it has a café, a gas station and a general store. Hell, most of the people who are *born* around here leave. And it's been my experience that Rossiter women—'' his eyes raked over her as if she were wearing a tiara and glass slippers instead of a pale yellow T-shirt and jeans ''—city-bred and addicted to champagne and Nordstrom's, are about as likely to stick around as a snowball in June.''

For a minute Glory stared at him blankly, wondering if he realized how much he'd just revealed about the breakup of his marriage. Then, the irony of the situation struck her.

She swallowed an irrational burst of amusement. That Logan Bradshaw should disdain her because he assumed she was rich, when Jack had rejected her when he'd found out she wasn't, was laughable. In point of fact, it had taken all of Glory's resources to buy her way clear of her employment contract with Waylan Arabians; the only things of any worth she had left were the two horses in the trailer hitched to the Cherokee.

Her amusement fled as the remnants of her pride went to war with her newfound sense of caution. On the one hand, she wanted to look this tall, handsome man in his ink-blue eyes and claim to be as rich as Croesus. Judging by his expression, such a declaration would secure his dislike and guarantee he kept his distance, which would, she told herself firmly, suit her just fine.

But on the other hand, she refused to lie; like it or not, she and Logan Bradshaw were partners and she put a high price on integrity, starting with her own. "Not that it's any of *your* business," she said to him, "but it's Melanie's side of the family that's well-off. Not mine. And as for Nile—" She gave a dismissive shrug. "I've lived in a lot of different places. I like small towns."

His expression hardened. "I like my privacy."

"We should get along just fine, then," she said, refusing to be intimidated.

Speculation replaced some of the exasperation on his strong, handsome face. "Look, Ms. Rossiter, if it's a matter of money—"

Glory could feel herself tense. "No," she said

flatly. "It's not. I make my own way, Mr. Bradshaw. I have for a long time. Despite what you think, I'm not afraid to work." She turned abruptly and started back toward the trailer, wondering why with men it always seemed to come down to money. "If you'd just tell me where you want me to put my horses, I'd like to get them unloaded. They've had a long drive."

He bit off a low, exasperated curse. "Lady, you aren't paying attention." With his longer stride, he caught up with her effortlessly. He reached out, cupping her shoulder to swing her back around. "I'm telling you I—"

His voice stopped abruptly as they stared at each other in a moment of mutual astonishment. As if his hand on her shoulder were a conduit, sexual awareness blazed between them, hot, fierce and consuming. It was so intense that for one mad instant, Glory actually envisioned black satin sheets, passion-flushed skin, and incredibly erotic acts that up until now, she hadn't even known she knew about, much less wanted to try. Wide-eyed, she stared at Logan, shocked by her extraordinary reaction to his touch—and so awash in desire she couldn't seem to breathe.

It took the shrill, unexpected blast of a truck horn to shatter the spell. With a muffled gasp, Glory took a hasty step back in the same instant that Logan snatched away his hand. "It sounds like you're being paged," she said shakily, still trapped in the depths of his deep blue eyes.

He tore his gaze from hers. "As a matter of fact—" he examined his watch "—I've got to get the boys to the school bus." Only the faintest darkening of color high on his cheekbones gave any indication he wasn't as composed as he seemed. That, and his newfound fascination with his Timex.

"Don't let me stop you," she said quickly, dismayed when she happened to glance down and discovered her hands were shaking. She quickly clasped them behind her back. "Just tell me where you want me to put these guys and you can be on your way."

His head jerked up, and whatever momentary awkwardness he'd felt was swallowed by renewed anger. "You just don't give up, do you?"

"Nope," she said with a lightness at odds with her quivering insides.

His eyes turned so dark they appeared almost black. He opened his mouth, but another impatient blare of the horn forestalled whatever he'd meant to say. He gestured curtly at the barn. "There are a pair of empty stalls at the far end."

She started to turn away. "Thanks."

"Don't think you've won, princess," he warned softly. "I'll be back."

She forced herself to face him. "I'll be here." Then she deliberately turned her back on him and pulled the pin from the trailer latch, swinging the left half of the door open.

Out of the corner of her eye she saw him stiffen, but a third trumpet of sound pierced the morning air, recalling him to the time. His shoulders rigid, he swiveled on his heel and stalked away, his long legs carrying him swiftly up the curving, tree-fringed drive and out of sight.

Glory turned to watch him go with a huge sigh of relief.

His thoughts churning, Logan reached the dark blue pickup idling at the side of his house in record time.

He yanked open the passenger door and climbed into the cab, settling next to his six-year-old son Christopher who was, predictably, dozing. His nephew Josh was poised behind the wheel. "So go," he said to the teenager. The fourteen-year-old wasted no time putting the truck into gear, and they shot off down the graveled road.

Staring blindly out the window, Logan took a deep breath and tried to get a handle on his agitation. Damn Gloryanne Rossiter anyway! He didn't want her here, and he'd hoped that once they'd met face-to-face and she saw how strongly he felt, she'd bow to his wishes and leave. But had she? Hell, no—and the knowledge made him seethe.

He already knew his hands were tied legally; his lawyer had advised she was within her rights to reside at Columbia Creek and that any legal action Logan took to remove her would be expensive and probably doomed to failure. And try as he might—and he'd been trying mightily for more than a week—he couldn't think of another way short of murder to make her go away. His hostile reception sure hadn't fazed her. Damn pigheaded woman!

Christopher shifted and snuggled closer to his side. "'Lo, Daddy," the child murmured sleepily.

Logan automatically brushed back a tendril of the little boy's golden hair, a bit of his tension receding with the gentle movement. "Morning, champ," he replied, only to discover when he glanced down that his son had sunk blissfully back to sleep.

A fleeting smile carved a faint slash in his cheek. No matter the state of the rest of the world, he could always count on Christopher to know the correct priority of things, he reflected.

His tension retreated another notch and he was able to reconsider his encounter with Gloryanne more calmly. Now that the impulse to throttle her had subsided somewhat, he realized that she wasn't at all what he'd expected.

She was younger, for one thing; younger and smaller and a whole lot less tough-looking than he'd imagined. When they'd talked on the phone, she'd been so brisk and businesslike he'd envisioned a tall, angular woman closer to forty than twenty-five. Yet she wasn't actually very big at all, although there was a certain strength in the easy way she held herself.

She sure as hell didn't look tough, either. She reminded him of a fawn, with her big, dark eyes, her straight little nose, and that thick mane of honey-colored hair that had been pulled back in a ponytail. She wasn't beautiful, but still… That disturbing moment when he'd touched her rushed into his mind.

Annoyed, he pushed it firmly away, dismissing it as an aberration. Some men might find her attractive, he conceded, but not him. Beyond the fact that he resented like hell her pushing in where she wasn't wanted, there was something about her that he found decidedly annoying. Perhaps it was her composure. Such a small, soft-looking woman shouldn't be so self-possessed, so poised. From the minute their eyes had met in the murky shadows of the barn, he'd felt irritated and out-of-sorts, as if his skin had suddenly grown too tight, and he didn't like the sensation at all.

And if that wasn't enough to seal his dislike, there was Josh.

Logan's tension returned full-force as he finally admitted that the driving force behind his opposition to Gloryanne's presence was his apprehension over his nephew's reaction to it. Deserted by his own mother as an infant, Josh had idolized Melanie even though she'd paid him scant attention. He'd been devastated by the divorce, but by the time Logan realized how deeply his nephew was being affected, it had been too late; the boy's hurt over what he saw as another abandonment had solidified into an angry distrust of women, which had only recently begun to abate. And which, Logan was afraid Gloryanne, with her connection to Melanie, would revive.

He shifted on the hard bench seat, and a rustling sound in his pocket reminded him that in addition to Ms. Rossiter, there was another little matter he and Josh needed to discuss—as much as he wished they didn't. "Seems the security alarm on the barn got turned off last night," he said, deciding he might as well get it over with.

As he expected, Josh looked instantly wary, darting him a quick, measuring glance before turning back to concentrate on the road. "Really?" the boy said with exaggerated nonchalance. "Are you sure you didn't just forget to set it? I mean, you are getting awfully old." The truck picked up speed as they rumbled down a slight grade.

Logan felt a reluctant stab of admiration for his nephew's nerve. "Thirty-three is hardly senile, Josh," he said dryly. "Besides, I did set the thing. Someone else turned it off—I think when they went in to get these." He dug into his pocket and brought out a crumpled pack of cigarettes and a handful of half-smoked stubs he'd found stuffed behind the grain barrel in the tack room. Joshua watched from the corner of his eye, but didn't say a word. "I figure you forgot to turn the alarm back on when you left," Logan said quietly.

Knowing his uncle had him dead to rights, the teenager flushed guiltily. He made an elaborate, offhand shrug. "Sorry."

Careful not to disturb Christopher, Logan twisted to stare hard at his nephew. "Sorry? Dammit, Josh, you know the rules. Cigarettes are off limits to begin with—but to light up in the *barn?* Barn fires are quick and deadly—a horseman's worst nightmare come to life!" Logan gave an involuntary shudder before he could stop himself. His expression turned harsh. "Hell—I can't stop you from smoking if you're bound and determined to experiment, but at least have the sense to do it someplace else."

The boy's shoulders rose defensively. "I said I was sorry!"

"Well, use your brain, for God's sake!" Logan said fiercely. He struggled to regain his composure, taking a deep breath and blowing it gustily out before slumping back on the seat. There was a protracted silence while Josh slowed the truck to navigate a series of large potholes. Finally Logan asked, "Why, Josh?"

Josh slanted his uncle a glance, then looked away, a dull red flush rising on his tanned young cheeks. After another long reign of silence, he said awkwardly, "There's this girl. Jennifer Sykes." His tone turned wistful. "She's about the most beautiful girl I've ever seen."

Great, Logan thought with a mixture of relief and despair, cursing Gloryanne's timing. It was the first time Joshua had admitted an interest in the opposite sex. "And?"

"We have the same study hall, and she smiles at me all the time." Josh gave a heartfelt sigh. "I want to ask her to the Harvest dance but I'm afraid she won't go with me."

"Why not?"

Josh slanted a quick glance at his uncle. "Because she's a sophomore and I'm just a lousy freshman."

"Ah." Logan considered it for a minute, then mused aloud, "So you thought you'd take up smoking. That it'd make you look older?"

"Yeah." Forgetting his embarrassment, Josh turned eagerly toward Logan. "A lot of the seniors smoke. I thought maybe if she saw me…" He trailed off at the look on his uncle's face, then had the sense to look sheepish. "Dumb idea, huh?"

"Yep," Logan said without any heat. He cocked his head. "Is this girl a flirt?"

Joshua shook his head decisively. "Nah. She's popular, but she's nice, too. She doesn't have a rep for leading guys on."

"Then why do you think she smiles at you?"

For a minute, the boy looked perplexed. It was obvious he'd been so caught up in his own insecurities he'd forgotten to consider the girl's feelings. Finally the hint of a smile touched the corners of his well-shaped mouth, so much like Logan's. "I guess maybe it means she likes me."

"You're not totally repulsive, you know," Logan said mildly. Unlike Christopher, who had inherited his mother's blond hair and brown eyes, the resemblance between Josh and Logan, who were both tall, dark-haired and blue-eyed, was striking and often re-marked on.

Josh's smile grew briefly wider. "Yeah, maybe," he said. Then as quickly as it had come, his smile evaporated and he turned to Logan and said earnestly, "I really am sorry, Uncle 'Gun—about the smoking, I mean. It won't happen again, I promise."

This time Logan could hear the honest contrition in the deep, young voice. "Forget it, Josh."

"No, I mean it. I know how hard you've been working the last few months, what with the last payment coming due, and I'd never forgive myself if I screwed things up—"

"Josh," Logan interceded softly. "Forget it. Besides, there's something else we need to discuss." He gazed out at the apple trees; they were a sea of green since the harvest had been completed the previous week. He cleared his throat. "You remember I told you that Melanie's cousin called?"

Just as Logan had feared, at the mere mention of his ex-wife, the boy's entire demeanor changed. His slender young body stiffened, his expression turning wary. "Yeah?" he said carefully. "What about her?"

Logan said a mental imprecation at the boy's sudden guardedness, his arm tightening reflexively around Christopher. "Her name is Gloryanne Rossiter and she's here."

"Here? I don't understand." Josh braked as they reached the blacktopped county road where the school bus stopped.

"She came this morning," Logan said steadily. "She's going to be staying for a while."

Josh's face, which had been so animated when he'd

been talking about the girl he liked, froze. "For how long?" he demanded.

"I don't know," Logan said honestly.

"Can't you make her go away?"

"Like I explained before, she owns part of the ranch," Logan said, concealing his own considerable frustration. He leaned over and gave the boy's shoulder a squeeze. "I know you don't like it, but it's going to be okay—"

Joshua shrugged his hand away. "Yeah, sure," he said, jerking open the truck door as the bus rumbled into view.

"Josh—"

"She'd just better stay the hell away from me and Chris," his nephew said vehemently, grabbing the younger boy's backpack as well as his own and launching himself out of the truck. Logan watched him go and again cursed Gloryanne's timing.

Sighing, he turned his attention to his son. "Wake up, sleepyhead," he said softly, giving Christopher a gentle nudge. "Time to go."

The little boy's eyes promptly popped open. He gave a giant yawn, stretched with languid grace, and slid dutifully across the seat in Josh's wake. "You 'member the M & M's for my lunch, Daddy?" he asked sleepily, completely oblivious to the lingering tension in the air.

Logan nodded. "Uh-huh. Packed them last night."

"Good." The first-grader sent his father an endearing smile, then climbed out of the truck, trailing unhurriedly after Josh toward the big yellow bus, pausing in the open doorway to wave. "'Bye, Daddy," he called. He sent Logan another smile. "I love you."

And with that he disappeared inside, while Logan's heart clenched at the contrast between his son's sunny, trusting expression and the angry hurt he'd seen reflected in his nephew's eyes.

He got out of the truck and rounded the hood, climbing in on the driver's side. *Gloryanne Rossiter better watch her step,* he thought fiercely as the bus rolled away with a belch of black smoke. *Legal or not, if she does one thing to hurt either of my boys, I'll throw her off Columbia Creek so fast she'll still be airborne when she reaches Montana.* And with that he slammed the door, put the truck into gear, and drove away in a spray of gravel.

Two

Glory stood uncertainly on Logan's back porch.

Like hundreds of other rural farmhouses dotting central Washington, his house was a plain, two-story clapboard structure, rectangular in shape, with a steeply pitched roof, back and front porches, and a large detached garage. The only thing to distinguish it was a spectacular view of the river.

Unless, Gloryanne corrected, you counted the mess.

Having spent the morning at the barn, she couldn't help contrasting its spotless order with the chaos on the porch, which at some time in the past had been enclosed to serve as a utility room. At least, judging from the mounds of laundry piled everywhere, Glory assumed that was its function; she had yet to actually locate the washer and dryer, but she guessed they

were somewhere beneath the clothes and other para-
phernalia strewn everywhere.

From her vantage point in front of the wire-mesh
screen door, what she could see of the kitchen looked
even worse. Pots and pans were heaped in the sink,
dirty dishes were stacked on every imaginable hori-
zontal surface, and the remnants of what looked to be
last night's dinner vied for space on the table with
several open boxes of cereal and a *Space Invaders*
comic book lying in a puddle of spilled milk. There
was a cage of white rats sitting on top of the stove,
a stack of cut-up magazines piled haphazardly in the
far corner and a bicycle pump hooked through the
refrigerator door handle.

All in all, it looked worse than the pictures of
Baghdad after Desert Storm.

None of which appeared to bother Logan, who was
sitting at the cluttered kitchen table, his brow fur-
rowed in concentration as he made notations with a
pencil in what appeared to be an account book.

Glory raised her hand to knock, then hesitated, not
wanting to startle him. "Hello?" she called instead.
Immersed in the stark reality of being nearly twenty
grand shy of the final twenty-five thousand dollar payment he needed to pay off the loan on the ranch,
Logan was slow to react. Frowning down at the fig-
ures, it was a moment before he looked up, and when
he did his distraction turned instantly to irritation
when he saw who was interrupting him.

As if I don't have enough problems. After he'd
dropped off the boys, he'd made what was supposed
to have been a quick trip to Moses Lake to look over
some horses. It had turned into a wild-goose chase
that had eaten up his entire morning, so that now he

was behind schedule. Although it was only eleven,
he'd already put in a six-hour day—and he still had
a hell of a lot to get done before nightfall. In addition
to his regular work—feeding, maintaining, training
and exercising the twenty-odd horses he currently had
on board—he needed to clean out the loft so he'd
have space for the winter hay that was being delivered
tomorrow, and get the sprinklers moved into the east
pasture so he could irrigate. Even though it was the
end of September, the temperature had hit the low
eighties yesterday. It was cooler today, but he
couldn't afford to take chances with his grazing land.
He needed the grass for forage; at close to a hundred
dollars a ton, hay was too precious to feed year-round.

For a minute he simply sat there, exhausted by all
the things clamoring to be done, remembering how
nice it had been when he'd had some help—and wondering why he couldn't even take a half hour for a
bite to eat and a quick look at the books without *her*
showing up.

He gave Gloryanne a long, slow look. "What do
you want?"

"May I come in?" she asked in that calm, unruf-
fled manner that grated on his nerves.

He closed the account book with a snap, suddenly
realizing that if she stuck around he was going to have
to fill her in on his financial situation—and hating the
thought. He gave a less than gracious shrug.

She opened the screen door and slipped inside.
"You had a phone call. When nobody answered here
at the house, I picked up down at the barn. It was a
man named Jeb Wright. He said to tell you he can't
make it tomorrow, but that unless he hears from you
differently, he and his son will bring the hay next

Tuesday.'' Message delivered, she took a step toward the table, only to stop when she discovered she'd stepped in something sticky.

Well, at least I don't have to worry about getting the loft done, Logan thought, watching in secret amusement as she took another step and found the new section of floor was gummy, as well. He knew the place was a wreck, but he was damned if he'd apologize. Right now all his energy—and every dime he could scrape together—had to go toward the payment coming up. If he didn't pull that off, he wouldn't have a ranch, much less a kitchen, with or without a dirty floor.

Still, as he got up to get another cup of coffee, he found himself remembering this morning and the stiff-necked way Gloryanne had said, ''I'm not afraid to work.'' *Yeah, well, she probably never pictured this. It'd serve her right if I treated her like a partner—and since I'm doing all the heavy stuff, she could pitch in around here.*

The thought stopped him in his tracks. Of course. It was so simple, so perfect, he wondered why it hadn't occurred to him before. It was the obvious answer to getting her to leave. He'd just give her what she was asking for—a taste of the responsibility that came with ownership.

In his experience, responsibility was something women didn't rush forward to embrace. He could barely remember his mother, who'd died when he was four, but the other two women who'd been instrumental in his life sure hadn't shown him too much. His older sister Annie had taken off when Josh was just an infant, leaving Logan to cope as best he could, and after her there'd been Melanie, who'd shredded the fabric of his life like a pair of sharp scissors.

They'd met in Seattle through a mutual acquaintance, had a whirlwind courtship and married in a matter of weeks. The minute the sexual haze between them had cleared, it had been obvious they'd made a mistake. Melanie had hated the isolation of Columbia Creek, the unrelenting nature of ranch work, and Logan's commitment to raising Josh; she'd refused to even try to make things work. The only good thing to come out of their marriage had been Christopher, born forty weeks to the day after their wedding. The divorce had been final in forty-one.

Logan's eyes narrowed as he considered Gloryanne. She wasn't exactly built like a workhorse, and he experienced a moment's uneasiness for what he was contemplating. But then he recalled the look that had been on Josh's face that morning and his brief uprising of conscience retreated. He'd do whatever it took. "You want a cup of coffee?" he asked.

Glory shot him a glance of pure shock, then looked away, embarrassed by her reaction when he was making an effort to be civil. "Sure."

He rinsed out a mug. "Cream or sugar?"

"Black's fine." He held it out and she wrapped both of her hands around the oversize mug. Taking a sip, she winced; the stuff was strong enough to use as paint stripper. Wondering if she was endangering her internal organs, she took another sip and took a surreptitious look around, deciding the room might actually be pleasant if it was cleaned up. The walls were painted pale blue, the countertops were white, there was a big double sink, fairly new appliances and lots of windows. The color of the linoleum remained a mystery.

Logan poured himself a fresh cup of coffee and sat back down. "There's an apartment over the garage where you can stay," he announced. "It used to be the housekeeper's."

Again Glory had to mask her surprise. "Thanks." She couldn't help but wonder at his sudden turn-around. It didn't make sense, not when he'd been so direct about not wanting her here.

"There's no kitchen, so you'll have to eat with us."

"Oh." Now she understood. She stared fixedly at her boots, cursing her sometimes inconvenient sense of humor as she tried to decide what would get her first. Botulism? Or ptomaine?

He gestured at the chair across from him. "Why don't you have a seat." It wasn't a request as much as an order, but since she was curious to hear what he was going to say next, she did as he asked, perching on the edge of the spoke-backed wooden chair he'd indicated.

"If you're going to stay here," he said, turning his cup around and around in his strong, long-fingered hands, "you're going to have to work."

Well, of course. She'd had a job of some sort since she was thirteen; it had never occurred to her that by coming here that would change. Naturally she expected to work in the stables, but she wondered if he'd be offended if she also offered to help with the house. It would be nice to have a real house to take care of for a change, she thought wistfully, even one that was probably on the health department's condemnation list.

"With my foreman out, I've got all I can handle taking care of the ranch and the stock."

She stifled a sigh. Obviously he needed her full-time in the stables. "I'd be glad to help," she said honestly. "And I think you'll be pleased with my experience. I've spent the past year with Waylan Arabians, training and showing their horses, and before that I—"

"I'm not talking about sitting on a fancy horse looking pretty," he interrupted coolly. "I break and train horses for a living, yes, but for pleasure riding and trail work—not for the show circuit. What I do here, Ms. Rossiter," his tone became lightly sarcastic, "isn't for ribbons or trophies or applause. I turn out nice, steady riding horses for everyday people—not flashy highbreds for rich girls to show off."

Both his look and his tone stung, and it took every ounce of Gloryanne's control not to defend the Arabians she so passionately loved—or to protest his low opinion of her skills when it was based on nothing more than his antipathy. But she held her tongue; she'd learned early on about proving herself. You had to earn respect; proclaiming your own worth seldom worked. "So what *would* you like me to do?" she asked neutrally.

He made a vague gesture that encompassed the room and beyond. "Maybe you haven't noticed, but since my housekeeper quit, things have gotten a little disorganized."

A little disorganized? It was like saying the Leaning Tower of Pisa was a "tad" off plumb, and all of Gloryanne's instincts told her to beware. She took a closer look at his handsome face, and realized there

was something other than dislike in his indigo eyes—
something that resembled anticipation.

"I thought maybe you wouldn't mind cleaning up
a bit," he went on blandly.

The man expected her to protest, she realized.
Heck, he expected her to *fail*. It was on the tip of her
tongue to ask him why, when a quick mental review
of their earlier conversation provided the answer.
He'd all but told her this morning that he considered
her to be about as useful as teats on a boar.

You don't have to prove anything, she reminded
herself. *It's not like before, with Jack—and the others.
You have as much right to be here as he does.*

Yet in her heart, she knew that wasn't true. Logan
Bradshaw had earned his right to be here, while she'd
been given hers. But still, did that give him the license
to judge her? It wouldn't kill him to lighten up, or to
give her a chance, yet that didn't seem likely to happen. Unless...maybe what he needed was to have his
preconceptions shaken a little.

"So?" he prompted.

She took a swallow of industrial-strength coffee. "I
guess it'd be all right," she said slowly. "There is
one thing, though."

"I thought there might be," he said complacently.

"Could I do the cooking, too?" She watched in
satisfaction over the rim of her cup as he appeared
momentarily nonplussed.

"Can you cook?" he asked finally.

"Yes. But..." Again, she hesitated, inwardly
amused when his expression subtly brightened.

"But what?"

"But I want to take care of my own horses, too.
And I'd be glad to help with yours."

"In addition to doing the cooking and cleaning?" he queried.

"Yes."

"Ms. Rossiter," he said carefully, "do you have any idea of what's involved…just in taking care of a house?" In the instant before it vanished, she actually thought she saw a flicker of concern in the depths of those blue, blue eyes.

"Not really." She made it a point to look slowly around the room before bringing her gaze back to his. "But then, apparently neither do you."

That did it. His jaw tightened, he stood up abruptly, picked up the account book and disappeared into another room, which Glory assumed must be either his office, or his bedroom. When he returned, he handed her a key. "That's for the garage apartment," he explained.

"Then we're agreed?"

He stalked toward the door, plucked a battered straw cowboy hat off the top of the coatrack and settled it on his dark head. "Princess," he drawled, "I wouldn't miss the next few days for the world." He paused at the door. "Now, if you'll excuse me? I've got some pipe to set. There's meat in the freezer—I like dinner by six." The screen door snapped shut with a sound like a pistol shot as he left.

Glory stared after his disappearing back. "A few days?" she repeated softly, slowly shaking her head. "Not on your life, Bradshaw. I'm here for the duration." And then she stood, tossed the dregs of her coffee in the sink, took a long look around—and wondered what on earth she'd gotten herself into.

Birds twittered in the loft as late afternoon sunshine spilled through the high windows of the barn. Enjoying the heat on her tired muscles, Glory gave a good-natured groan. "I think I'm getting old," she told Faisana as she brushed the mare's glossy chestnut hide. "And I know I'm getting decrepit." The small, pointed ears on the elegant head flicked alertly toward the sound of her voice, and Gloryanne smiled, realizing that although she was exhausted, it'd been a long time since she had felt this content.

She'd made a good start on the kitchen. Although there was still plenty to do, she'd cleaned up the worst of the mess, discovered that the floor was white with blue and beige speckles, and started supper, making a batch of cinnamon muffins and putting together a hunter's stew.

That last had been easier said than done, since there'd been nothing but a package of Popsicles in the refrigerator-freezer. It had taken her a while to realize that there must be a second freezer somewhere. By the time she had, and had managed to unearth the chest freezer buried beneath a pile of laundry on the utility porch, she'd been so annoyed with Logan for not being more specific that she'd been tempted to wash a load of his clothes and stash them inside it.

In the end, her better sense prevailed, but the idea, giving as it did new meaning to the term *freeze-dried,* had gone a long way toward restoring her sense of humor.

Once things were under control in the kitchen, she'd checked out the garage apartment, which consisted of a sitting room, bedroom and bath. Although it was by no means luxurious, it was better than a lot of the places she'd lived in over the years, and she'd been feeling pretty good when she'd walked down to the barn, intending to unhitch the trailer from the Cherokee and drive back up to unpack.

But it was just too nice a day for any more indoor tasks. Humming under her breath, she reached for Faisana's bridle, glad she'd decided to go for a ride instead. She had more than an hour before she needed to check on dinner, and she could get settled in after that; since she didn't own much in the way of clothes or other personal items, it wouldn't take long.

As she bridled the mare, she could hear Je'zhar stomping around his stall down the corridor, clearly disgruntled that he wasn't the one she was taking out. She smiled. After her confrontation with Logan, she was just too tired to contend with another headstrong male, and the young stallion was definitely that. He was mischievous and demanding, and it required all of her wits to stay one step ahead of him. "Cool your jets, big boy," she called, her smile widening when he answered with a snort of disgust. "Tomorrow, when I'm rested, I promise we'll go exploring." She turned Faisana toward the door, only to come to an abrupt halt when she found Logan standing there, his expression holding all the menace of an imminent thunderstorm. "What's the matter?" she said instantly.

"I'll tell you what's the matter," he said, closing the distance between them in a few long strides. "My nephew Joshua is coming unglued—and all because of you!"

"Oh," she said, taken aback. She wondered what she could have done already to make him this mad.

She didn't have to wait long to find out. "What

the hell did you do to his science project?'' he demanded.

"His science project?'' She tried to recall if there
had been anything that had looked even remotely sci-
entific in the kitchen, and drew a complete blank. "I
suppose I washed it,'' she said in an effort to mollify
him. "Unless…'' She felt a sudden stab of alarm.

"Unless what?'' he persisted.

He was a big man, and he was so close he towered
over her. She resisted the urge to take a step back.
"He wasn't growing penicillin or something, was he?
I mean, I did throw some pretty scary stuff out of the
fridge—''

His eyes bored into her. "Why don't you knock
off the innocent act? Josh put a lot of time into teaching those rats to run a maze, dammit, and—   ''

"Rats?'' *Uh-oh.* Cleaning their cage and putting it
in the living room had apparently been a big, big mistake. She tried to figure out what could have gone
wrong. Had she used the wrong kind of bedding? Or
set them in a draft? Or maybe that stuff she'd thought
was mold in their water tube had actually been a special dietary supplement. Or—

She was so busy hypothesizing it took a minute for
what he said next to penetrate.

"Did you cook them to get back at me? Is that
why you left the pot out in plain sight?''

Her conjecturing slammed to a stop. Cook them?
He believed she'd *cooked them?* She automatically
opened her mouth to tell him in no uncertain terms
that the only pot she knew about was the one holding
the beef stew—and then she snapped it shut. He definitely needed a lesson, she thought.

Her eyes darkened dangerously. "So," she said deliberately. "You caught me."

"Caught you?" he said incredulously. "You're *admitting* it?"

Taking advantage of his momentary shock, she clucked to Faisana and maneuvered the mare around him, heading outdoors. "Sure." She grabbed a handful of mane and swung herself effortlessly onto the mare's bare back. Gathering up the reins, she twisted to face him. "Obviously, I can't put one past you. After I scrub floors, I always fricassee rodents. Then I feed them—" her voice dropped "—to the unwary."

She leaned forward and went on in a confidential whisper, "And if you think that's bad, you should see what happens when I vacuum." She gave him a wicked smile. "If you have a cat, Bradshaw, you'd better hide it."

And before she was tempted to say another outrageous word, she gathered the reins, pressed the mare into motion and sent her flying out of the yard.

Three

By the time Gloryanne guided Faisana back to the barn it was dark. Catching her lower lip between her teeth, she stopped the mare in the pool of light from the fixture above the big sliding door and carefully slid off.

The minute her left foot hit the ground she knew she was in trouble. Agony shot through her ankle, making her head spin and her knees start to buckle. She sucked in her breath at the pain—only to let it out in a startled yelp as seemingly out of nowhere a pair of strong, warm hands reached out to steady her.

"Oh!" she exclaimed as Logan stepped out of the shadows.

"What did you do to yourself?" he demanded, swinging her into his arms and shoving open the barn door with one broad shoulder. "Get thrown?"

Glory produced a ghost of a smile. "I beg your

pardon.'' She tried not to think about the clean, male scent of him or the surprisingly natural way it felt to be in his arms. ''I'll have you know there hasn't been a horse with the poor taste to throw me in years.''

He made a rude sound. ''That so?'' He walked briskly down the darkened corridor toward the tack room. Stepping inside, he set her down on an old burgundy leather couch at right angles to the door. His sharp blue eyes surveyed her cloud of disheveled hair, the bruise marring one smooth cheek, and the tear in the left knee of her jeans. Seeing that she was shivering, he shrugged out of his denim jacket and wrapped it around her, ignoring the immediate stirring in his blood the sight of her chill-hardened nipples produced. ''So what happened? Trip over your mouth?''

''Very funny.'' The oversize jacket was still warm from his body, and she tugged it around her, luxuriating in the infusion of heat as she shook her head self-deprecatingly. ''As it happens, I was leading Faisana and I stepped in a hole. Stupid of me.''

He eased down on the floor in front of her. ''Yeah, well…
there's a lot of that going around.''

Their eyes met, and she realized that he was trying, however awkwardly, to apologize for his earlier behavior. ''Forget it,'' she said softly. ''It's been a long day—for both of us.''

The sight of him kneeling at her feet was disturbing. As if operating independently of her brain, her eyes swept over him, moving up the muscled planes of his chest and past the tanned column of his neck to settle on the beautifully delineated curves of his mouth.

Uncomfortable with her scrutiny, he frowned at her legs, encased in an old pair of English knee boots. "So where does it hurt?" he asked gruffly.

"It's my left ankle," she said, trying to convince herself her sudden shortness of breath was caused by the pain and not his proximity. Yet she found herself wondering what it would feel like to press herself against that hard torso, to nuzzle her cheek against the warm satin of that strong throat, to trail kisses from it to the corners of that beautiful mouth.

Her breath quickened as in her mind's eye she saw him rising above her, his broad chest slick with sweat, the hair on his thighs silky against her nakedness....

He rocked back on his heels and stood. "I guess we'd better get you over to County and have a doctor take a look at you."

His statement snapped her back to reality and she realized he'd started for the door. "Logan—" What on earth was happening? It was her ankle she'd strained, not her brain.

He swung back around. "What?"

"Forget it. I—I can't afford it, and besides, I'm fine."

He stared at her impatiently. "Why don't you just drop the needy pose, okay? And you're not all right, you're white as a sheet."

She braced a hand against the arm of the couch and struggled to her feet, managing to take two halting steps before she teetered to a stop. "See—" she said stubbornly, even as the floor started to rush up to meet her.

Logan dived for her, locking his arm around her waist and twisting so that he was beneath her by the time their combined momentum slammed them to the ground. Stunned by the sudden impact of the fall, he lay flat on his back and struggled to catch his breath with Glory sprawled on top of him.

She slowly raised her head from his chest. "Are you all right?"

He stared at the ceiling. "Oh, I'm just great," he said caustically.

She could feel heat surge into her cheeks. "I'm sorry. I guess I'm a little light-headed. I don't think I've eaten today." She paused, remembering what had sent her fleeing in the first place—and was struck by the absurdity of it. "What about you?" she asked in a voice that was suddenly unsteady.

He raised up on his elbows. "What?"

She couldn't help the smile that suddenly lurked at the corners of her mouth. "Had any unusual m— meals lately?" she stuttered, only to dissolve into laughter at the expression that came over his face.

She slipped sideways into the notch created by his outstretched arm and his body, and he could feel every soft curve cradled against him as the laughter gently rocked her. Her breath fanned across his cheek and the faint smell of apples filled his head. Later, he would tell himself he'd brought his hand up to push her away. He certainly didn't plan on cupping her cheek or stroking the rounded sweetness of her chin with his thumb—nor was he ever sure afterward how she came to be in his arms, the laughter gone, her velvety eyes wide as she stared up at him.

He kissed her then, a kiss that was unashamedly potent and blatantly male, and Glory gave a little sigh, molding herself to him until their bodies were pressed tight, mouth to mouth, thigh to thigh, breast to chest.

His hard, chiseled lips brushed hers like heated silk,

and she clung to him, feeling as though she'd plunged off a darkened cliff and was falling endlessly down a black satin abyss, her only chance for safety the anchor of his arms. With suddenly restless fingers she traced the sculpted muscles in his back, sketching them as they bunched across his shoulders, stretched along the firm indentation of his spine, smoothed down into his narrow buttocks and his strong, lean thighs. The taste of him on her mouth, the warmth of his lips... She felt disoriented, swept away by heated yearnings and liquid longings that made her ache for more.

Logan felt swept away, too, and his heartbeat soared on a rush of adrenaline as sparks exploded in the nerves beneath his skin. Sheer, sensual excitement roared to life deep in his gut and his control blazed away on a lick of desire more intense than anything he'd felt since he had his first woman a lifetime ago.

With a guttural sound that was totally male, his tongue claimed hers, exploring the sweetness of her mouth, stealing her breath, robbing him of reason. She was so soft, so warm. The fragrance of her hair and skin wafted around him, soap and sunshine and flowers, and he was suddenly burning up.

Longing washed over him. Longing for her softness, her heat, her touch.

His very urgency set off warning bells in his head. He wanted her too much, and after his disastrous lapse of judgment with Melanie, he'd sworn to never again let passion rule his head. His control balanced on a razor's edge, he wrenched his mouth from hers and rolled away, shuddering for breath. In the far reaches of his mind echoed the alarming idea that something incredible had just happened, and he struggled to dismiss it.

To his right, Glory lay limply where he'd left her, hating his control—even as she was grateful for it, since it was plain she didn't have any. Her lips throbbed; her entire body yearned for more of his touch. She wanted to fling herself on top of him, feel the hot velvet of his skin against hers, taste again the distinctive flavor of his mouth.

He didn't even like her, she reminded herself, touching her tongue to her kiss-swollen lips. With his looks, he could have any woman he wanted—and probably did. She remembered Jack's words, the ones she'd overheard him saying so casually to one of his friends. *Glory's a plain little thing, but that's good; women like her don't expect very much.*

The memory burned through her, pushing her to her knees and onto her feet.

"Hey!" Logan said in surprise. He surged upright, reaching out to steady her when she swayed. "Are you all right?" he asked hoarsely, still striving to control his aroused body.

She forced her voice to steadiness. "I'm fine. But I need to take care of my horse." She was so intent on escaping him, she forgot entirely about her ankle.

"Dammit, don't—!"

But it was too late. With a total disregard for the consequences, she stepped down hard on her left leg—and fainted at his feet.

Stubborn little fool, Logan thought, making his way up the back stairs of his house with Gloryanne cradled in his arms. Pausing in the middle of the utility porch, he glanced down as the light from the kitchen spilled across her face, illuminating the curve of her cheek, the thick sweep of her lashes, the lush contour of her mouth, and something uncomfortably like tenderness stirred to life where it was buried deep inside him.

He shoved it back down, wondering what the hell it was about this woman that punched holes in his usually impregnable defenses. One moment he wanted to strangle her, and the next he wanted to strip her bare, stroke her everywhere and discover what made her shiver.

It was guilt, he tried to tell himself. It was natural that he should feel bad about making those foolish accusations since they'd resulted in her getting hurt. It wasn't like him to go off half-cocked the way he had and he was still puzzled by his behavior. Faced with Josh's near hysteria, he'd never even thought to ask how thoroughly the boy had searched for the damn rats, he'd just seen the pot on the stove and gone charging down to the barn to confront her.

His mouth quirked a little as he recalled how she'd flung that tale about fricasseeing the critters at him. Another woman would have protested her innocence or cried in a bid for sympathy. But not this one. She'd looked like a ruffled little cat, but she'd stood up to him—he had to give her that.

"Uncle Logan? That you?" The inner screen swung open and Josh was outlined at the door, more curious than alarmed.

Logan stiffened, embarrassed to be caught standing there in the dark. "Yeah," he said gruffly, making his way into the house. "It's me." With Josh at his heels, he carried Glory across the kitchen and into the living room, which had a plain red brick fireplace, several tall, narrow windows, beige carpet, serviceable furniture, and the same air of neglect as the rest of the house. Skirting a football lying in the middle of the floor, he just narrowly missed tripping over Christopher who was stretched out on his stomach, coloring.

The little boy immediately sprang to his feet and began bombarding Logan with questions. "Is that Mommy's cousin, Glory? Why're you carrying her? How come her jeans are ripped? Is she dead?"

"Yes," Logan said, "this is Glory. And no," he laid her carefully on a blue and brown sofa that had seen better days, "she's not dead." Despite his sharp words, he gave Christopher, who'd come to stand next to him, a reassuring pat. "She hurt her leg. When she tried to walk on it, she fainted."

"Oh." Christopher studied Glory. "She's pretty," he pronounced. Joshua made a rude sound from his vantage point on Logan's other side, but Christopher ignored him and cut right to the heart of the matter. "So why're you mad at her, Daddy?"

"I'm not," Logan said, thinking he'd better watch himself. He wasn't in the mood to discuss his suddenly rampaging sexuality with either boy. He searched for a plausible explanation for his gruffness. "I'm worried," he said finally. *Yeah—that she won't clear out before you give in to the desire that's riding you.*

"What're you worried about, Daddy?"

Logan stifled a sigh, wondering if there was another creature on earth as persistent as a six-year-old. "I'm going to have to take her boot off, Chris," he improvised, "and I'm afraid it's going to hurt."

"Oh." The single word held both sympathy—and

bloodthirsty small-boy anticipation. Despite himself, Logan felt a smile struggle to life inside him.

Before it could reach his lips, Gloryanne's lashes fluttered up, her eyes widening as she found herself the focus of three sets of eyes, two pair as blue as a robin's egg and one as brown as her own.

"What happened?" she asked, dredging up a faint smile.

"You fainted," Logan said brusquely.

A wash of pink stained her pale cheeks as it suddenly came rushing back to her—their kiss and her panicky feelings afterward. Feeling more than a little foolish, she held herself still, gathering the strength to sit up while waiting for the nausea to subside.

As if he could read her mind, he said roughly, "Would you please just lie there? I'd prefer not to scrape you up off the floor again if you don't mind." He nodded curtly at each of the boys. "This is my son Christopher," he said, "and that's Josh."

"Hi," she said.

Logan turned to the older boy, whose resemblance to him was startling. "Do you have something to say to Ms. Rossiter?"

The boy, who'd been watching Glory with an expression of studied indifference, turned sullen. "Uncle Logan—"

"Just do it," Logan said flatly.

Staring at a spot to the right of her nose, the teenager mumbled quickly, "Thanks for cleaning out my rat cage. I'm sorry I jumped to the wrong conclusion."

"No problem," Glory said, more than a little confused by the undercurrents she could feel swirling between Logan and Josh.

"Now," Logan said to his nephew, "would you go down to the barn and put Ms. Rossiter's horse away? And lock up?"

Even though it was phrased like a question, there was only one correct response, and Josh made it—grudgingly—as his uncle ushered him toward the kitchen. The minute they were out of sight, Glory sat up.

A grin split Christopher's face. "Daddy's gonna yell if he sees you." He plopped down on the sofa beside her and confided in a loud whisper, "But don't worry, 'cuz even if he says he's gonna, he'll never spank you."

"Ah." For a fleeting moment, Glory actually thought about that. And then, disturbed by the image it evoked, she concentrated on the throbbing in her ankle, which felt as if it was being systematically struck by a sledgehammer. "That's a relief." *In more ways than one.* She studied Logan's son. He was as beautiful as a Rubens's painting, with a confident way of holding himself and a winsome intelligence in his soft brown eyes.

"Yeah. Sometimes he tries to sound mean, but he's really not. He even draws pictures of our cat for me—"

So Logan *did* have a cat. Gloryanne fought a grin.

"—on my napkins, when I take my lunch to school. I'm in first grade," he said importantly, "and our cat is called Bunnymuffins."

"I see." Glory tried to sound suitably impressed, but her imagination was captured instead at the thought of Logan—virile, macho Logan—owning anything named Bunnymuffins, much less sketching it for a child's entertainment. For some reason, the information was disturbing.

"Are you really my mom's cousin?" Christopher asked.

"Yes," she said, glad for the change of subject. "That makes us cousins, too, you know."

His face lit up with interest. "Really?"

"Mmm-hmm." She screwed up her face and pretended to think. "First cousins, once removed, I think."

"I don't remember my mom," he confided matter-of-factly. "She left when I was real little. Daddy says she loved me a lot but she got too lonesome at the ranch to live with us."

Glory didn't know what to say. She'd only met Melanie once, at the funeral for Glory's parents. Her recollection was of a very beautiful but clearly spoiled youngster who'd coolly made note of the poor way Gloryanne was dressed, despite the fact that Glory had just lost her mom and dad. When she'd been notified of her unexpected inheritance, Glory had wondered fleetingly if it was Melanie's extravagant way of making amends for that long-ago unkindness.

"Was she pretty?" Christopher asked, his young voice wistful.

Gloryanne pushed the past back where it belonged. "She was beautiful," she assured him.

"Josh's mom was pretty—I've seen her picture. She looked just like Daddy, only she was a girl. That's 'cuz she was Daddy's sister—"

"That's enough, Christopher," Logan said, striding back into the room. A nerve ticked along his jaw, but he didn't say anything more, not even when he noticed that Gloryanne was sitting up, her booted feet

resting on the floor. Instead, he unceremoniously
dumped everything he was holding—a pair of scissors, a roll of surgical tape, a pair of clean towels,
something that resembled pruning shears and a plastic
bag filled with ice—onto the end table at Glory's
right.

He picked up the shears and her eyes rounded with
apprehension. "What do you think you're going to
do with those?" she asked, temporarily forgetting
Christopher.

"I'm going to cut off that boot," he said brusquely.

She raised her hands as if to hold him off. "Not a
chance, cowboy." She gestured at the supple leather
of her well-worn boots. "These are my favorites."

He shrugged. "So buy another pair, princess."

She shook her head stubbornly. "Just pull it off."

His eyes drilled into her, and she knew she had
Christopher's presence to thank when all Logan said
was, "It'll hurt—a lot."

She met his navy gaze steadily. "I know. But I
really do like these boots, and besides..." She sent
him a challenging look. "I'm tough. Remember?"

His expression closed. "Fine. Christopher," he
said, his gaze gentling when it rested on his son, "it's
time for you to get ready for bed, champ."

"Aw, Daddy," the little boy said, looking crest-
fallen.

"Come give me a kiss," Logan said firmly.
"Josh'll be back in a minute to tuck you in, and I'll
be along after a while."

The child appeared to be on the verge of protesting
some more, but reconsidered when he saw the resolve
on his father's face.

"'Kay," he said with exaggerated despondency.

Still, he went eagerly into his father's arms, giggling as Logan whispered something in his ear. He bussed his father's cheek. "I love you, too, Daddy."

Logan gave him a gentle hug and then spun him around and gave him a playful swat on the seat of his pants. "Good night, scamp," he said firmly.

"G'night, Daddy. G'night, Glory," he said, trudging out of the room with exaggerated reluctance. They heard him start up the stairs, and knew to the moment when he thought himself out of earshot because he began to jump exuberantly from step to step, sounding like a whole herd of boys all by himself.

"He's wonderful," Glory said softly.

"Yeah, he is," Logan said shortly, his tone making it clear he didn't intend to discuss his son with her. His eyes probed her pale face. "I may not be able to get that boot off, you know."

It was on the tip of her tongue to tell him she couldn't afford to replace this particular pair of boots. Except that he probably wouldn't believe her, anyway. "Just do it," she instructed. "This won't be the first time."

Going down on one knee, he positioned himself before her and gently grasped her slim, leather-shod foot in his hands. "I thought you said you hadn't been thrown in years?" he said, one hand supporting her ankle as the other applied pressure to the heel of the boot as he attempted to slide it off.

The pain was considerable. Beads of perspiration popped up across her nose and nausea rolled through her, but unlike earlier in the barn, this time she was prepared. Her hands curled into fists, her nails cut into her palms—and from somewhere she found the strength to dredge up a shaky smile. "Come on, Bradshaw. You work with horses.'' She gasped as the boot finally started to come free, then continued doggedly through gritted teeth, ''You don't have to be on 'em to get hurt. Don't tell me you've never been nipped or kicked or stomped.''

He shook his head. ''Not me.'' His gaze met hers meaningfully. ''Nothing—and nobody—stomps on me.''

The boot came off in his hands and Glory slumped back against the couch cushions, light-headed from the sudden release of pressure on her ankle. She was too weak to protest as Logan came to his feet and in one lithe, smooth action shifted her sideways so she was once more lying down. ''This time don't get up,'' he ordered, reaching for the scissors and deftly slicing up the inside seam of her jeans to the knee before she could say a word. Folding the denim up, he peeled down her sock, whistling soundlessly between his teeth when he saw the bruising at her ankle. Gently, the whisper softness of his long fingers directly at odds with the grim look on his face, he examined it. ''Well,'' he said finally. ''I don't think it's broken.''

''I told you it's just a sprain,'' she said, sucking in a breath as he used a towel to brace her leg before packing the bag of ice around the bruised, puffy skin.

Straightening, he looked down at her and said curtly, ''You might as well plan on spending the night on the couch.''

''No,'' she said instantly. The idea was too tempting; to be in the same house, wrapped in the dark warmth of night, with Logan simply a room away....

He busied himself picking up Christopher's abandoned coloring book and crayons. ''I don't like it any better than you do, but it makes the best sense. It'll save me the trouble of having to leave the kids in the middle of the night to check on you.''

Well, it was obvious *he* wasn't suffering any delusions of rampant lust, Glory thought crossly. And put that way, what could she say? The set of his jaw made it clear he wasn't likely to change his mind— or pay any attention to her insistence she didn't need watching over. And all of a sudden, she was too tired to argue, the pain in her ankle and the eventful day making her eyelids heavy. "Okay," she said.

He looked momentarily startled at her easy capitulation before he started purposefully out of the room. "I'll get you something for the pain and a pillow and blanket."

She yawned, snuggling down into the couch, the thick tangle of her eyelashes making feathery shadows on her cheeks. "Thanks."

By the time Logan returned, she was fast asleep.

Carefully setting down a glass of water and some aspirin, he let the bedding under his arm slide to the floor as he stood looking down at her. Desire slashed through him like a knife at the sight of her curled like a kitten on her side, one slim hand tucked beneath a flushed cheek, her full pink lips moist and slightly parted.

The slam of the screen door jerked him back to the moment. He turned slightly to see Joshua standing in the kitchen doorway. "You get things taken care of?" he asked.

"Yes," the boy said. "I even remembered the alarm."

Logan ignored the querulous note in the teenager's voice. "Thanks."

Josh shrugged. "It wasn't as if I had a choice," he

reminded Logan. He paused and a muted note of excitement crept into his voice. "Have you taken a look at that stallion of hers?" An excellent rider, he shared his uncle's love of horses, and when Logan shook his head no, he mimed a silent whistle. "You'd better," he said. There was a faint glimmer of interest in his eyes for the first time as he looked past Logan to the small figure on the couch. "That's one hell of a horse." As if catching himself, he suddenly looked uncomfortable. "Well, good night," he said, and without another word, he turned and headed for the stairs.

"Good night," Logan returned. He reached down and repositioned the ice pack, propped it against the cushion back, and covered Gloryanne with the blanket before turning off all but one of the lights.

He was almost to the door when her voice drifted across the night to wrap around him like a midnight caress. "Thank you, Logan," she murmured sleepily.

Logan had to set his teeth as a sudden urge to join her on the couch slammed into him. For just an instant he imagined rolling her beneath him and settling himself in the notch of her silky thighs. He pictured the way her slender arms would tangle around his neck and her mouth would open hotly under his, and he could almost hear the soft little cries of hunger she'd make....

Heat curled through his belly. Heat and need and—

No. He sucked in air and said something very soft—and very savage. *No.* Heat he could handle. He'd proven that earlier tonight.

But he'd sworn never to need another woman again, and even the idea that he'd think of the word in conjunction with Gloryanne Rossiter was more than disturbing.

It was alarming.

Squaring his shoulders, he told himself his sudden sense of panic was foolish, a reaction to the financial stress he was under and the unpredictable events of the day.

He might want Gloryanne Rossiter. But he didn't need her. Need made a man vulnerable and left him wide open to disappointment, and he'd had enough of that to last a lifetime.

And with that thought set firmly in his mind, he walked unhurriedly out of the living room and padded across the kitchen and into his own room.

Only he didn't stop there. He kept right on going, his face set as he continued on into the bathroom to jerk open the glass shower door and turn the water on as cold as it would go.

He yanked off his boots.

And then, still fully clothed, he stepped inside— only to discover that despite his determination to will it other-wise, he could barely feel the icy water for the pounding of his heart.

Four

Balancing the laundry basket on her hip, Gloryanne hesitated in front of Logan's bedroom door, her hand on the doorknob and her stomach in knots, and wondered why she was so reluctant to go inside.

He was just a man, she chided herself. So what if she felt an attraction for him more explosive than the eruption of Mount St. Helens? Over the past week and a half, he'd made it abundantly clear the feeling wasn't mutual. In fact, ever since the night they'd shared that devastating kiss, he'd gone out of his way to avoid her.

And it wasn't as if she was going to walk in and demand he make mad passionate love to her. The last thing she needed was the kind of complication a fling with Logan Bradshaw would bring to her life. She was just going to deliver his laundry and do a little cleaning, and then she'd be out of there.

Besides, he was down at the barn helping the vet patch up a yearling who'd tangled with a fence and managed to come out the loser.

As much as it shamed her to admit it, it was that last fact that finally gave her the impetus to turn the doorknob and step inside. She'd only gone a few feet, however, when she stopped and her eyes widened in surprise.

Whatever she'd been expecting—those black satin sheets she'd envisioned the first day they met, mirrors on the ceiling, a king-size heated water bed—this wasn't it.

There was an old scuffed bureau, a rectangular window with a roll-up shade and a double bed on a metal frame. Next to the bed was a narrow bedside table, which sported an alarm clock and a ginger jar lamp missing its shade. To her right was the closet and the door that led to the bathroom.

That was it. There were no curtains, no rugs, no mirrors—she glanced quickly at the ceiling—anywhere. No pictures or mementos or books. No magazines. Not a television or a stereo or even a radio in sight. There wasn't even any of the bric-a-brac that usually collected in a man's room; change from pockets, a hairbrush or comb, a dish left from a late-night snack, a bottle of after-shave. The atmosphere was utilitarian in the extreme—and Glory hated it on sight.

With a shake of her head, she set the laundry basket on the floor and crossed to the rumpled bed, stripping off the limp beige sheets as she puzzled over her reaction.

She already knew that Logan worked fifteen to eighteen hours a day, which hardly left him the time to indulge in interior decorating. And the rest of the house was hardly a pleasure palace. So why should it bother her so much that his room was so bleak?

Not for the first time, she found herself speculating about the lack of a woman in his life. It was clear, from several innocent remarks Christopher had made, that Logan rarely if ever dated. And she had firsthand knowledge that there was nothing wrong with either his instincts or his sex appeal. If he wanted companionship all he'd have to do was mention it, and she was sure every unattached female in the Pacific time zone would be on his doorstep, vying for the job.

So why *was* he alone? Even if his marriage to her cousin hadn't been a happy one, these days half the population survived divorce. It wasn't as if it had happened yesterday, after all. It had been six years.

She unfolded a clean bottom sheet and wrestled it onto the mattress, her thoughts marching inexorably on.

It had something, instinct told her, to do with Josh.

Unlike Christopher, whose trusting nature and innate openness had allowed the two of them to quickly establish an easy rapport, Josh, just like Logan, avoided her whenever he could. And when he couldn't, he was as prickly and unapproachable as a porcupine.

The one exception was when she worked Je'zhar. Then he actually sought her out, although he was careful to stay in the background where he thought he wouldn't be seen, his expression as he watched her work with the stallion a mixture of longing and wariness and defeat, as if he wanted something badly but knew it could never be.

It was a look that Glory recognized, because it reminded her of herself as a child, and how it had felt to think, deep down inside, that you'd been judged and come up short, with no way to redeem yourself— and no chance to, if you could.

She smoothed a wrinkle out of the sheet, feeling the familiar tightness inside as she remembered the look of pity that had been in the social worker's eyes when the woman had informed her that Aunt Louise and Uncle Frank didn't want her. And as easy as that, the old litany of questions arose to taunt her one more time.

Why? What's wrong with me? Why don't they want me?

At twenty-six, she knew, intellectually at least, that the fault had been her aunt's and uncle's. Although her father and Melanie's had been brothers, the two men had never been close, and her uncle had obviously felt no compulsion to take on a shy little girl who, unlike his beautiful Melanie, preferred jeans to party dresses and horses to proms.

She shook her head, marveling that after all these years the rejection still stung. Yet it did. As did the memory of what had followed, when she'd lived in nine different foster homes in six years.

Which was a major difference between her and Josh, she thought as she unfurled the top sheet with a satisfying snap, then let it drift down onto the bed. Josh was neither unwanted nor alone; he had an uncle who loved him as fiercely as ever a father could, and who'd go to the mat for his nephew as quickly as he would for his son.

Still, she lived here now, too, and Logan's hostility was more than enough. And if there was a chance her horses could help to ease the tension between herself and Josh, she intended to take a shot at it. As a matter of fact—

"What are you doing in here?"

She whirled, her heart in her mouth, to find Logan barring the doorway, his feet bare and his shirt hanging open. "Oh. It's y—you," she stammered, unable to tear her eyes from his chest. It was a great chest, beautifully sculpted and liberally covered with a vee of dark curls above a stomach that was hard as a rock and washboard flat. The entire impressive expanse was toasted a warm shade of bronze. He must work bare-chested, Glory thought, feeling a little dazed.

He took a step into the room. "I believe I asked you a question."

Her eyes jerked to his face, and it occurred to her to wonder what he *thought* she was doing. Stealing his sheets? "I'm changing the linen and then I'm going to clean."

"Oh." As if he couldn't help himself, his eyes flicked from her to the bed and back again. His expression was odd, the skin across his cheekbones stretched taut, as if he were operating under some sort of galling restraint. "Well, do you think you could clear out for a minute?" he said brusquely. "I'd like to change."

She had him mentally stripped in an instant. His shoulders would be wide and the color of teak, his back long and lean, his legs straight and strong. She tried to remember if she'd washed a pair of cutoffs or a swimsuit for him, her mind speculating madly about where that golden tan would run out. At his waist? Or would he be bronzed everywhere except for—

"I'd sort of like to do it this year, if you don't

mind," he said sarcastically. "I told Christopher he could go with me to deliver a horse this afternoon, and I thought I'd meet the school bus."

"Oh." She sent the message from her brain to her feet to move, but they ignored her, while her eyes kept trying to get a better look inside his open shirt. Mortified by her inability to control her body, which seemed to have been overtaken by some sort of hormonal autopilot, she struggled for a plausible reason to explain why she was still standing there. "Did you sell a horse?"

He gave her a shuttered, unfathomable look, then shrugged deliberately out of his shirt. "Yeah. I finally found a taker for little Afternoon Delight." The shirt fluttered to the floor.

It took her heart right with it. *Good Lord, was she that obvious?* She flushed and forced her gaze to the ground.

"She's that little sorrel with one white foot."

"Right." She dragged in a breath. Now that she wasn't looking at him, she was feeling a great deal more herself—except that she still appeared to be permanently rooted to the floor. "Well, that's good."

Clearly out of patience, Logan stalked past her, stopped by the dresser to pull out a pile of clean underclothes, then tramped toward the bathroom. "I'm going to take a shower," he growled. "Do you think you could manage to be out of here by the time I come out?"

"Absolutely," she assured him even as some devil made her wonder what he'd do if she offered to wash his back.

As if he could read her mind, Logan muttered a

heartfelt curse and slammed the door with a resounding bang.

Bemused, Glory turned slowly back to the bed, her gaze zeroing in on Logan's lone pillow. Frowning, she glanced from it to the quilt she'd set aside when she'd stripped the bed, thinking idly that even though it had been unseasonably hot lately, it was still getting cold at night, and he could probably use another blanket.

The thought jarred her out of her inaction. With a quick look at the bathroom door, she dashed to the linen closet and grabbed another blanket—and, feeling oddly defiant, another pillow and case—and returned to the bed, which she quickly remade. Then she dusted and polished the nightstand and dresser, washed the window, set his clean clothes on the freshly made bed, gathered up the dirty linens and, when she heard the shower shut off, made a mad dash for the door.

But even as she fled to the kitchen, she couldn't deny the sense of restless dissatisfaction that followed her down the hall, or the reluctant admission that it was due only in part to the barrenness of Logan's room.

Je'zhar, the young Arabian stallion Glory had raised from birth, was the color of burnished mahogany, with a black mane and tail, four black socks and a lineage that could be traced back for more than a century.

Like any young prince of the blood, he could be extremely demanding, and the minute Gloryanne set foot in the barn, he began to trumpet a demand for an immediate audience. Glory smiled at the sound;

although she loved Faisana, there was a special place in her heart reserved solely for Je'zhar.

Opening his stall door, she watched in appreciation as he danced to the far side of the stall, as light on his feet as a shadowboxer as he tossed his elegant head and snorted disdainfully to demonstrate his displeasure with her recent lack of attention.

"Hey, Zharie," she said, pulling an apple out of her coat pocket and suppressing a smile as the stallion's entire body quivered when he caught the scent of the ripe fruit. "Come see what I brought you."

If there was one thing larger than Je'zhar's pride, it was his appetite, and in seconds he forgot his pique and was practically on top of her, deftly snatching the apple from her palm with a scrape of his big strong teeth.

She soon had the stallion brushed and tacked up in a lightweight flat saddle and a simple snaffle bit. Then she led him into the arena where she hooked the lunge line she'd slung over her shoulder around one of the railing posts before swinging into the saddle.

It was like straddling a high-energy wire. As she cocked her heels down in the stirrups and lifted the reins, she could feel the coiled tension quiver through his graceful frame, and the instant she gave the low-voiced command, he leaped into an energetic walk as if he'd been released from a spring-loaded catapult. They began their usual routine, going through each gait to warm up, then practicing figure eights before moving on to more complicated dressage movements.

It was nearly forty minutes later before she happened to glance up and catch sight of Josh standing unobtrusively in the shadows. She reined in, turning Je'zhar in the boy's direction. "Hi," she called, trying to sound surprised to see him. "How was school?"

He shoved his hands into his pockets and gave an eloquent shrug. "All right," he said coolly, avoiding her gaze.

"Do you have your boots on?" she asked, as if she couldn't plainly see them.

He glanced down at his feet. "Well...yeah." The look he turned on her now was nominally more curious than hostile.

She slid off the stallion. "Then would you mind giving me a hand?"

"Me?" he asked in surprise.

She leaned down and rubbed gingerly at her lower leg. "Uh-huh. My ankle hurts and this guy is still full of himself."

Like a moth drawn to a flame, the teenager drifted closer, until he was standing only a few feet away. "What do you want me to do?"

"Ride him, if you don't mind a lunge line," she told him. The lunge line, a feather-light nylon ribbon an inch and a half wide by sixty feet long, could be attached to the bridle and used to run Je'zhar through his paces from the ground. Although Glory had observed Josh exercising Logan's horses and knew he was a good rider, Je'zhar was so quick and powerful he could be as hard to contain as a hurricane. The lunge line was a necessary safety device, since she didn't intend to take any chances with either Josh or her beloved stallion.

"You want me to ride him?" Josh's expressive face mirrored the disbelief in his voice.

"If you wouldn't mind."

"Heck, no! I mean..." He cleared his throat, reaching out to reverently stroke the stallion's neck, and Je'zhar's nostrils flared as he inhaled the boy's scent. The horse gave a snort and sidled closer, lipping the teenager's shirt.

"Be careful he doesn't nip you," Glory said dryly, handing the surprised boy the reins as she walked past him to retrieve the lunge line from the fence. "It's all those treats you've been feeding him. The way to this guy's heart is definitely through his stomach."

Trying to fend off the greedy Arabian's search for food, Josh flushed at her casual reference to what he'd thought had been his secret. "How'd you know?" he mumbled. Turning, she flashed him a grin. "Elementary, my dear Bradshaw. A combination of the dwindling supply of carrots in the fridge—and his utter delight at seeing you. Usually, he's leery of strangers."

"Oh." The boy glanced uncertainly at the English saddle. "Do I have to use that sissy thing?" he asked.

"Yes." She gave him a quick measuring glance before she began to adjust the stirrups for his longer legs. "Actually, I think you'll like it once you get used to it. I've watched you ride your uncle's horses and you have light hands and a nice seat. You'll be surprised at how much better you can feel the horse this way. But," she cautioned, "you have to pay attention. Unlike a Western saddle, there's nothing to hold on to on this sissy thing, and Zharie will leave you treading air if you aren't careful."

"I will be," he said. Despite his attempt to sound casual, anticipation lit his eyes like sparklers on the Fourth of July, and Glory felt a surge of pleasure at being the one to put it there.

She snapped the line onto the stallion's bridle, then

motioned the boy up. Once he was settled in the unfamiliar saddle, she showed him how to hold the reins of the English bridle, one in each hand, different again from the Western manner where both were held in a single hand, which had evolved from the need to free the other one to swing a lariat—or wield a gun.

Once Josh was ready, she moved away, playing line out as the boy and the horse moved around her in ever-widening circles.

The next half hour was one of the most enjoyable that Glory had ever spent. She had a natural affinity for teaching, and Josh proved an able student, quickly adjusting to the change in riding style, although there were some hilarious moments as he tried to get the hang of posting, the English way of coping with the trot.

It wasn't until Glory glanced at her watch and realized it was time for her to get dinner together that she called a halt.

"That was great." Face flushed, Josh glowed with satisfaction as he swung out of the saddle, too exhilarated to remember to be aloof. "Can we do it again sometime?"

Delighted that he'd ask, Glory smiled. "Sure. You did really well," she told him sincerely, coiling the lunge line and handing it to him. She ran the stirrup irons up the leathers so they wouldn't bang against Je'zhar's sides, then started from the arena. "Nobody watching would guess it was your first try at a flat saddle."

"You think so?" he asked, following along.

"Absolutely. You should've seen me the first time. I was seventeen, and every time the horse went one way, I went the other."

He looked at her in surprise. "Seventeen? But...you ride so well. Like you've been doing it forever."

"Thanks." With Josh keeping pace, she moved unhurriedly out into the sunshine, heading for the barn. "I rode Western when I was little. My family had a few acres and we always kept a horse—my mom loved them. But I didn't learn to ride English until later, from a woman who bred and trained Arabians. I'd had some trouble and Bev and her horses really straightened me out."

Glory had spent her last year in foster care with Bev Cartwright, then stayed on to be the older woman's assistant up until a year ago, when failing health had forced Bev to retire. From there she'd gone to work for Waylan Arabians—where the boss had thought to get an outstanding horse and a hardworking trainer for the relatively cheap price of a wedding ring.

"Yeah, well, at least you knew your mom and dad," Josh said, kicking a pebble out of his path. "My mom never said who my dad was—before she deserted me." He glanced at her out of the corner of his eye, as if trying to gauge the effect of his words.

Glory fought her surprise. She knew from Christopher that Josh was Logan's sister's child, but she'd assumed that his mother had died; not once had it occurred to her to think otherwise.

Realizing she was being tested, she didn't say anything for a moment, carefully considering her response as they entered the barn and stopped before the tack room door. It was cool inside after being out in the sun.

"She didn't want me—and she still doesn't," he

said abruptly. "And she was never married. That makes me a bastard."

Glory handed him the reins. Wise enough to know better than to try and dispute his first part of his statement, she responded to the last. "Is that supposed to shock me?" she asked, moving past him to uncinch the saddle.

"Well, doesn't it?" he demanded.

Knowing she was taking a chance, she still decided that nothing less than the truth would do. "Frankly, I don't care if you were dropped to earth by aliens from outer space," she told him. "I won't pretend that there aren't some people who'll think less of you because your parents weren't married, but I'm not one of them." She paused, then said bluntly, "What bothers me more is that it sounds like you don't appreciate what you have."

For a second, he looked incredulous. From the expression on his face it was clear he'd expected sympathy, and Glory surmised that was the usual response from people to whom he revealed the details of his parentage. Then, when it dawned on him she'd gone so far as to criticize him, his face reddened. "What's that supposed to mean?" he asked belligerently.

She shrugged. "It means I think you should spend more time being proud of the family you have instead of dwelling on the one you don't. It's pretty obvious your Uncle Logan loves you as much as any biological father could, and Christopher worships the ground you walk on. You should be glad you have them."

"You don't understand," he said truculently.

"Maybe not." Standing on tiptoe, she lifted the saddle from Je'zhar's back. "So explain it to me."

"You're just like my mom—and Aunt Melanie. Right now, you think it's cool to hang around with us, but pretty soon you'll get bored and leave!"

Now where had she heard that before? Obviously Josh and his uncle had more in common than she'd realized, including a "when feeling threatened, attack" conversational philosophy. She deposited the saddle on a peg inside the tack room door, picked up a currycomb, stepped back outside, and began to brush the stallion. "I'm not going to lie to you, Josh. I can't promise I'm going to be here five years or five months or even five days from now. Things are a little awkward between your uncle and me, and I don't know what the future's going to bring.

"But I can tell you this." She stopped and turned to face him, her eyes steady as she met his stormy gaze. "I'd like us to be friends, and that won't change, no matter where I live. And I'll always be straight with you—even if it makes both of us uncomfortable at times."

Still tense, he stared at her. "If I say I don't want to be your friend, does that mean you won't teach me to ride English?"

From the look on his face, she could see that he thought the answer was a foregone conclusion. She suppressed a sigh, cursing the circumstances—and the women—who'd put the bleak look in his eyes. "No. If you want to learn, I'll be happy to teach you."

There was a moment of stunned silence. "I still may not want to be your friend," he warned.

"Maybe not," she agreed, turning back to gently run the currycomb over Je'zhar's sleek hide.

Behind her, Josh shifted uneasily. "I just don't get

you," he said finally. "Why're you being so nice? What do you want?"

"From you?" she said softly, again stopping to look at him. "I want the same thing I'm willing to give. A chance, Josh, just a chance."

He stared at her, perplexed, and then said, so low she could barely make it out, "I just don't know, okay?"

And with that he spun on his heel and walked away.

Knowing that the best thing for now was to let him go, Gloryanne forced herself to say nothing, to stand silently by and watch as he disappeared from view.

And then she turned, resting her cheek against Je'zhar's warm shoulder as snatches of a similar conversation from her past came tumbling back, pouring out of her memory. She could hear Bev as if the older woman was standing in front of her, could remember the sternness of her voice, so at odds with the compassion in her eyes.

Let it go, girl. You can't always control what the world dishes out—but you can decide how to deal with it. If you get handed a bushel of lemons, it's up to you whether they sour your life or you find a way to make lemonade.

And her own voice, young and agonized and angry, so much like Josh's. *I don't know, okay? I just don't know.*

"But I do now," she whispered to Je'zhar, running a hand down his satiny neck.

The hard part was going to be finding a way to share the knowledge with Josh without putting him off—or incurring even more of his uncle's enmity.

Five

The early morning sun turned the dun-colored plateaus to gold. Sprawled in bed, Logan twisted onto his back, the muscles in his upper arms rippling as he bunched the pillows beneath his head.

Yawning, he watched the play of light across the ceiling, trying to decide whether it was the sunshine streaming through the window that had awakened him, or the tantalizing aroma of coffee.

Then again, he thought with a faint scowl, it might be the sound of muffled laughter that had interrupted his sleep; despite their obvious effort to smother it, he could just make out Christopher's childish giggle and Gloryanne's alto chuckle coming from the kitchen.

Even though he never would have believed it was possible, he had to admit that Gloryanne had more than risen to the challenge he'd tossed her. His house was so clean it all but squeaked, the laundry was always done, and if he didn't quit stuffing himself at the dinner table he was going to have to invest in some bigger jeans.

And as if that wasn't enough, she was easily the best stable hand he'd ever had. In addition to taking care of her two Arabians, she cheerfully did whatever else needed to be done, whether it was pitching hay, grooming horses, cleaning stalls or soaping tack.

He ought to be pleased. Hell, he ought to be doing handsprings.

But he wasn't, he thought darkly. As a matter of fact, if the truth were known, with every day that passed he felt more and more out of sorts, as if he wanted to punch someone.

Or—perhaps more accurately—as if he wanted to grab Gloryanne and haul her into his room for a long, sweaty session in bed. Yet, his antsiness wasn't only because things hadn't gone the way he'd planned. Or even because he was being painfully consumed by a lust he had no intention of fulfilling.

No, there was more to it than that. But what?

He pondered the question as he climbed out of bed, his toes curling against the softness of the throw rug that had mysteriously appeared, before he padded over to the bureau and hauled out a set of work clothes.

Perhaps, he thought, catching a faint scent of lemon wax as he looked down at his blurred reflection in the dresser, it was the way Gloryanne already seemed to be putting her stamp on things that was really bothering him.

He didn't even have to leave his room to see the evidence of that; it was right in front of him in the freshly polished dresser, and by the bed, where in addition to the rug to warm his feet there was also an extra blanket on the bed, and a second pillow to cushion his head. Just as there were gauzy curtains on the window and a pleated shade to cover his lamp. There was even some sort of plant with fuzzy leaves and pink flowers parked on one end of his dresser, for cripe's sake.

He paused on his way to the closet to grab his boots, listening as another low burst of laughter came from the next room. The sound went straight to his gut, and he added it to the growing list of things about Glory that were getting to him. Like her pervasive presence in his house, her laughter pulled at him, making him yearn for things he'd long ago decided he'd probably never have. Things such as kindness, companionship and someone soft and gentle to turn to in the night.

But the wanting only increased his frustration, reminding him of how self-defeating it was to wish for things that he'd learned were just a fallacy.

Because eventually, inevitably, she'd leave. She might be getting a kick out of taking care of the house, and the boys—and even him—for now, but he knew it would never last. He'd seen her on that stallion of hers and she was good—damned good, and he didn't believe she'd remain content at Columbia Creek for long, no matter what she said.

Sooner or later she'd get tired of all the work, become disenchanted with the kids, start to pine for all the amenities she was probably used to, and take off. And if, by then, he'd been stupid enough to let her get even further under his skin than she already was, where the hell would that leave him?

A glance at the clock jolted him out of his thoughts. Moving back to the bed, he sank down onto the mattress and yanked on his socks, staring stupidly at the dial as he realized he'd overslept.

He frowned. A mare with a bellyache had kept him up late last night, and by the time he'd come to bed he'd been out, asleep on his feet. But still, he would've sworn he'd set the alarm.

He reached hastily for his boots. Stomping into them, he stalked into the bathroom to scrape the beard off his face and decided, as he gazed sourly at his reflection in the mirror, that the only good thing about this day so far was that he didn't need to bathe.

He'd had so many ice-cold sessions in the shower lately that his skin was beginning to chafe.

"I give up!" Christopher cheerfully informed Gloryanne, who was standing at the stove, breaking eggs into the frying pan. The little boy was perched across from Josh on a chair at the kitchen table. "Why don't cannibals eat clowns?"

She picked up the pitcher of orange juice and poured some into his cup. "Because, silly," she scolded, her eyes twinkling as he began to giggle even before he heard the punch line, "they taste funny."

He gave a delighted laugh, then said instantly, "Tell me another one—please?" His brown eyes were liquid with entreaty.

Gloryanne hid a smile when Josh rolled his eyes. "I thought we agreed five jokes ago that one was going to be the last one."

"Pu—leeze," he begged.

She winked at him, then pretended to think. "Well,

I think I might—just possibly maybe—know another one.''

"Oh, boy," Christopher crowed.

"Oh, no," Josh moaned.

Christopher shot him a speaking glance before saying to Glory, "Tell me!"

Even though he might not look much like his father, Christopher definitely had the Bradshaw appeal, Gloryanne thought ruefully. Even so, she was determined to hold him off for a few minutes or she'd never get breakfast on. "First, you need to set your place. If I'm going to run you to school this morning, we need to get a move on."

"Okay," he said agreeably, grabbing the necessary items from the center of the table where she'd put them. "I can't believe you're really gonna drive us! It's gonna be so cool. We always have to take the bus 'cuz Daddy's always working. Can I sit in front?"

"I don't think Josh will mind. Will you, Josh?"

"Oh, please," the teenager said in a pained tone.

"Oh, good," Christopher said happily.

He was so eager—and so easy—to please. Glory was engulfed by a wave of tenderness as she glanced over at him and saw the earnest expression on his little face as he carefully put his napkin in his lap and industriously lined his silverware up in a tidy row. Place set, he looked up beseechingly. "Now will you tell me?"

She placed a platter of bacon in the center of the table, then moved back to the stove, picked up the frying pan and began to dish out the eggs. "You bet. What's Irish and stays out all night?" she asked, putting a stack of toast on the table with one hand and pouring milk with the other.

There was silence as the little boy pondered.

And then, out of the blue, Josh ventured, "Sinéad O'Connor?" naming the Irish rock singer known for shaving her head.

Glory's gaze flew to his face, trying not to stare as she actually saw a smile there. It was faint, to be sure, but it was a smile.

He'd grumbled no end when she'd rousted him out of bed this morning to help her do Logan's chores. And when she'd asked him to sneak in and shut off his uncle's alarm, he'd done it, but grudgingly, and only after darkly predicting a very bleak future for them both when Logan finally awoke.

Still, he *had* helped, and she must be doing something right if he felt comfortable enough to make a joke.

A very bad joke, she reminded herself. "That's not exactly the answer I had in mind, Joshua," she chided, feeling a thrill when his grin actually widened, if only by a fraction.

"So what is?" Christopher demanded around a mouthful of scrambled eggs.

"Don't talk with your mouth full," she said automatically. And then, "Sure you don't want to guess?"

He shook his head decisively. "No!"

"Okay, then. The answer is…Paddy O'Furniture."

Christopher promptly began to howl with laughter, while Josh gave a heartfelt groan. "Where do you hear these things?" he muttered.

"I never reveal my sources," she said, only to have

the amusement dancing in her eyes change swiftly to
wariness when Logan stalked into the room.

"Why didn't somebody get me up?" he demanded
into the sudden silence, snatching up a mug and pouring himself a cup of coffee. In his agitation, he
splashed as much of the hot liquid on the counter as
he managed to get in the cup.

Glory cursed the sudden uneven quality of her
pulse. "You needed the sleep." The understatement
of the century. He kept a schedule that would hospi-
talize a lesser man, doing hard physical labor day after day on a scant five or six hours sleep. And as she'd
stood in her darkened doorway last night and watched
him trudge up the drive from the barn, his shoulders
bowed with weariness, she'd come to the conclusion
that enough was enough.

Obviously he didn't agree. "Yeah?" The look he
turned on her was as wintery as a January night. "So
why don't you just amble on down to the barn, princess, and tell that to the horses? Of course, be prepared for some hoof stomping and stall kicking. They
tend to be decidedly unsympathetic on an empty
stomach."

"But Glory and Josh already fed them," Christopher said innocently.

The coffee cup froze midway to Logan's mouth.
"What?"

His son picked up a piece of bacon and took a
healthy bite. "Wasn't that nice, Daddy?"

Glory spooned eggs onto a plate and waved Logan
toward a chair. "Josh thought you could use a morning off," she said lightly, setting the plate down and
sending the teenager a warning look when he opened
his mouth to disclaim responsibility for the idea. "So

we took care of it. Do you want more coffee?'' She pulled the glass carafe from the automatic coffee-maker and poured him a refill without waiting for an answer.

Christopher sent his father a puzzled look. ''Aren't you gonna say thanks?'' he inquired.

''Thanks,'' he said, looking briefly at Josh before his gaze swung back to Gloryanne, following her as she moved around the kitchen, the economy of her motions belying the efficiency with which she got things done. ''You, too.''

''No problem,'' she replied, although he still looked far from pleased. Not that she'd expected gratitude or anything. But at the same time she hadn't expected him to look so…condemning, either. ''It was worth the price of admission just to watch Josh ricochet off the walls. I've never seen anybody take so long to wake up.'' She wiped up the coffee he'd spilled with a graceful sweep of her hand.

''Hey,'' the boy protested, ''not everyone gets up like they've been jump-started by a rocket launcher. You're so cheerful it's disgusting.''

''I like mornings.'' She whisked a plate of toast down next to Logan's elbow. ''Everything's so quiet. There's a sense of endless possibilities at the start of a day.'' Uncomfortably aware Logan was still watching her with that gimlet stare, she gathered the cooking pans and set them in the sink to soak before hastily drying her hands.

She walked to the coatrack by the back door, knowing she was taking the coward's way out—and not caring. ''If you guys would scrape your plates and put them in the sink,'' she said, pulling off the apron she was wearing and exchanging it for her old copper-

colored ski parka, "I'll load the dishwasher later."
She shrugged into the coat and zipped it up.

"But where are you going?" Christopher demanded.

"I'm going to go get my purse and warm up the
Jeep." She turned up her collar and flipped her ponytail out from under the back of the coat.

"But what about *your* breakfast?" he wanted to
know.

She shrugged and opened the screen door. "I had
a piece of toast." She smiled at the child with amused
affection. "And you'd better quit talking and hurry
up." She glanced at her watch. "I'll be back to pick
you up and load the cupcakes in ten minutes—so
don't dawdle."

She started across the utility porch, her footsteps
pausing as she heard Logan inquire, "Cupcakes?
What's that all about?"

Christopher's voice was bright with enthusiasm.
"It's for Columbus Day, Daddy." There was the
sound of a chair scraping back, and then a few seconds later Christopher said, "See? Mrs. Sandman
asked if anybody's mom wanted to help out and I
tolded her Glory would."

Logan's sigh was clearly audible. "Christopher…"

"It's okay, Daddy—Glory said so. She said anybody whose name was Christopher just had to help
out on Christopher Columbus Day. And see, she even
found these little flags to put on them so they look
like the *Nina* and the *Pinto* and the *Auntie Maria.*
Aren't they cool?"

Logan's response was drowned out by Josh's snort.
"That's the *Santa Maria* and the *Pinta,* squirt. Not
the *Pinto.*"

"Is not!" Christopher said indignantly.

"Is too," Josh came right back.

"Knock it off, you guys," Logan said.

Glory heard another chair scrape back, and then came the distinctive tap of Logan's boots, jolting her from her inaction. Flushing as she realized that what she was doing might be construed as eavesdropping if it was discovered by a certain person, she bolted out the door.

"What," Logan asked Gloryanne, "is that?"

It was midafternoon, and they were standing at opposite ends of the utility porch.

Poised just inside the outer screen door, Gloryanne cursed her rotten luck. Ever since the morning a few days ago when he'd had such an unsociable reaction to her doing his chores, she'd done a stellar job of avoiding him—and the confrontation she could sense was brewing.

Now, not only were they face-to-face without the comforting buffer of the boys between them, but he'd caught her red-handed at something she'd planned to discuss with him first—and confess to having already done later.

Not that she had anything to hide or that what she'd done was really wrong, she reminded herself, her posture straightening slightly. It was just that she'd wanted to ease into the subject and avoid another argument if at all humanly possible.

"Well?" With a lift of his chin, Logan again indicated the bundle squirming in her arms. One brow rose up, as well, in that way she was beginning to find annoying.

So much for her hopes and wishes. If the storm

gathering on his face was anything to go by, he was about to rain on her parade—in a sizable way.

Deciding to make one final stab at deflecting his burgeoning anger, she tried a little humor, glancing down as if she hadn't realized she was holding a puppy until he mentioned it. "This? Oh. This is Fred. We came to get some newspapers. For paper training." She paused, then said diffidently, "I hope you like dogs."

Logan eyed the puppy's generous proportions. "That isn't a dog. That's a pony," he said flatly, reaching for his hat, which was perched on the top of the dryer. Like the rest of the house, the appliance gleamed, but if Logan noticed, he didn't give any indication. His somber expression never changing, he settled the hat on his head and nodded at the puppy. "Where'd he come from? And what are you doing with him?"

"I got him at Nielsen's," she said, naming Nile's general store while secretly thinking it was a shame he'd covered up his hair. He had beautiful hair; dark and thick and shiny. In the bright sunlight, it gleamed like sable. "There were some things I needed, and when I went in, there he was. He was the last one left."

"I bet. Are you aware that the only dog Bridget Nielsen has is a Great Dane?"

"Yes. Bridget said she thinks the father was the Barnhard's dog." Staring up at her adoringly, Fred sucked a piece of her dark green T-shirt into his mouth and began to chew energetically.

Logan's mouth tightened. "Did she also happen to mention the Barnhard's dog is a St. Bernard?"

"She might have," Gloryanne admitted reluctantly.

He gave the puppy a critical stare. "He's ugly," he pronounced.

"He is not. He's cute."

"He's the color of mud, he's got beady eyes and legs like a stork, and his ears and his paws are the size of Frisbees. You call that cute?"

Hefting Fred a little higher in her slim arms, Glory shot Logan a disgusted look and marched toward the kitchen, even though he was rooted in front of the door like a tree trunk. "Beauty isn't everything."

"Yeah?" He gave a dismissive shrug, then crossed his arms over his chest and cocked his hips in a stance that shouted male authority. "I guess that's true. But in this case it doesn't matter—since you're going to have to take him back."

Glory started to sidle past him, only to stop when the meaning of his words penetrated. A stubborn glint flashed to life in the brown velvet hue of her eyes as they searched his. "I will not."

"I don't have time for a dog," he said stonily.

Her chin came up. "I didn't know you had one." She tried to ignore her awareness that his shoulders were twice as broad as hers, or that in his cowboy boots, he stood easily a full foot taller than she did in her old canvas tennis shoes.

"You know what I mean."

"No, I don't. Fred is my dog." It wasn't his size she found so disturbing, she realized unhappily; it was his nearness.

"Oh, that's just great." His voice was gathering steam with every word. "You come home with a puppy that Christopher's bound to fall in love with—

and when you finally get tired of playing *Little House on the Prairie* or whatever the hell it is you're doing, and take off, either my son gets his heart broken or I get stuck with a dog the size of a Mack truck." Hands on his hips, his blue eyes dared her to disagree.

But Gloryanne didn't rise to the challenge. "So we're back to that," she said, momentarily overcoming the extraordinary effect he had on her hormones to focus on his infuriating personality. She set the restless puppy on the floor and straightened to her full height. "Pay attention, Bradshaw," she said with quiet determination. "I'm not going anywhere. I live here."

"*Now,*" he emphasized.

"All right," she said, raising her hands in mock surrender. "Just to spare us another argument, I'll concede your point. I live here *now.* Which still doesn't give you the right to dictate whether or not I can have a dog, does it?"

He opened his mouth and then slammed it shut, his frustration evident as his jaw worked, and she pressed her advantage, determined to put an early end to the discussion. "Look, I get a little nervous in the apartment by myself at night, okay? I thought Fred would be some protection, as well as good company. And as far as Christopher's concerned, well, he could use a buddy, too. Maybe you haven't noticed, but he spends an awful lot of time alone."

Logan's entire demeanor changed. "I don't need you to tell me how to raise my son," he warned.

"I'm not trying to!" she shot back. "But somebody needs to say something. You spend all your time working—what about fun? Or don't you believe in that, either?"

"Now wait just one damn minute—" he began, only to have the rest of his statement drowned out by a loud, thrumming feline growl that sounded a lot like a B-52 throttling up for takeoff, followed by a high-pitched canine scream of terror, and then all hell broke loose as Fred hurtled toward Gloryanne in an explosion of motion, with Bunnymuffins the cat in hot pursuit.

For one electric second chaos reigned, and then Logan's voice lashed out. "Muff!" he warned. At the sound, the big orange tomcat froze in midair, did what looked to be an aeronautically impossible about-face, and streaked for the door, his body hitting the screen door with enough force to open it for his escape.

Whimpering, Fred trembled against Glory's legs, his entire body quivering from the close call. She bent down, trying to reassure him. "Poor little guy," she crooned, running her hand gently over the top of the cowering animal's bony head.

"Now that's what I call a protector," Logan said in disgust. "Hell, if he's afraid of Muffy, he'll probably faint dead away if we ever have an actual intruder."

"He's just a baby," Gloryanne said defensively as the puppy, exhausted by the close call, staggered over to the corner and collapsed. "And since you're so fond of vehicular comparisons, your 'Muffy' bears a close resemblance to a Volkswagen!" She whirled around to confront him.

In the same instant that she turned, Logan took a step forward, their movements coinciding to send her crashing into him so that she literally bounced off his chest. Off balance, she staggered back, until he shot out his arms and reeled her in, steadying her against

him. Her eyes flew up to meet his, and she was reminded of the night in the barn, and the way it had
felt to be cradled in his arms, so close to the satin-
over-steel strength of his body.

Suddenly it was hard to breathe. Her pulse accel-
erated; her head felt fuzzy; and to her chagrin, she
could feel the crests of her breasts blossom into aching arousal against the soft, worn cotton of her
T-shirt—and the hard-heat of his midriff.

They both went still, and then his gaze began to
drift down her body, drawn to the quivering softness
of her breasts. As his eyes locked on the raised cen-
ters, a pulse in his throat jumped to life, making
Gloryanne shiver.

As if monitored by an independent source, her
senses soaked up his deeply masculine scent of sunshine, leather and hard work, while her fingertips tin-
gled with the desire to smooth along his sun-bronzed
arms and under the edges of his shirt to feel the
sculpted hardness of his wide shoulders. "Logan,"
she said urgently.

His head came up, his expression unreadable, and
she realized she wanted him to kiss her again. Worse,
she wanted it more than she'd wanted anything for a
long, long time. And she wanted other things, as well,
sultry, sexy things she couldn't name but could only
envision—such as the damp heat of his mouth suck-
ling at her breast, and the strength of his hard, long-
fingered hands urging her against the length of his
masculinity.

The thoughts rolled through her like the hot rush
of a tropical tidal wave, heating her blood, making
her heart race, sending her swaying closer to him,

until another image intruded and she remembered the rest of what had happened that night in the barn.

His control. Her lack of it. And the decisive way he'd thrust her away.

She took a deep breath, remembered humiliation tangling with the desire pounding through her, and suddenly she was determined not to embarrass either of them by repeating an invitation he'd already declined. "I'll make you a deal," she managed weakly, praying to come out of this with some small amount of her dignity intact.

"Really?" he murmured, in that softer-than-velvet voice that never failed to send a tingle shooting down her spine. Shadowed by the brim of his hat, his eyes were nothing more than a glint of jewel-blue.

Before she could stop it, her gaze skimmed the chiseled contours of his lips and she could feel the strength seep from her knees as wild thoughts of passion persisted in ricocheting through her head. "If I leave, the choice is yours whether I take Fred or he stays. And if you decide to keep him, I'll pay for his food for a year." She swallowed. "How's that?"

He stared at her, and for the briefest of seconds she thought she saw a look of stunned disbelief in his eyes before his mouth tightened ominously. "What did you say?"

With a sudden wash of panic, she realized she wasn't entirely certain. There was just something about him that seemed to short-circuit her brain. She ran her tongue over her suddenly parched lips and tried to gather her composure. "I said," she began again, hoping to God that this time she'd make sense, "you can choose to keep Fred—or not, and—"

"I heard you," he snapped.

Perplexed, she watched as a flush of color blossomed high on his cheekbones, wondering what on earth she'd done now as the sapphire shine of his eyes darkened to cobalt. Abruptly he stepped away, and without the lean strength of his body to brace her, she nearly toppled to the floor. Not that Logan noticed; he was too busy striding toward the door. "Fine," he bit out.

"Oh. But—I didn't mean…" She trailed off, watching in confusion as he hit the screen with his palm, sending it crashing against the side of the house as he vaulted down the steps.

"Don't wait dinner for me tonight," he threw back over his shoulder. "I'll eat in Nile!" And without further explanation or a single backward glance, he marched to the pickup, yanked open the door, flung himself inside and went roaring out of the yard.

Glory glanced uncertainly from Fred, who was staring at her mournfully over his oversize paws, to the plume of dust left by Logan's passage, and back again. "What do you suppose that was all about?" she asked.

Fred gave a long, ululating moan.

Glory turned back toward the yard, watching the dust cloud settle slowly back to earth under the weight of the hot fall sun, and sighed. "I guess you're right, Fred," she said finally. "Men *are* like cats. Who can understand either one?"

Six

The sound of footsteps coming up the stairs to her apartment brought Gloryanne's head up. She glanced over at Fred, who was sleeping on a blanket in the corner. He didn't stir, not so much as an eyelash. So much for her "protection."

Smiling ruefully, she tossed aside the afghan covering her shorts-clad legs, and set down the romance novel she was reading. Scrambling out of the overstuffed rocker, she headed for the door, concern for the boys hastening her steps.

Everything had been fine when she'd left them half an hour ago. Christopher had been tucked in to bed and Josh had been hunkered down at the kitchen table, studying for a history test. There hadn't been any reason to hang around—or so she'd thought.

Now she knew a moment of panic as she wondered if she'd done the right thing by leaving. Maybe she should have waited until Logan got home. Maybe Christopher was sick or Josh had had an accident. Maybe—

"Hi." Logan stood, big and darkly beautiful, on the other side of the screen door. "Got a minute?"

He didn't look like a man whose son had unexpectedly contracted a raging case of beriberi or whose nephew had been hit by a bus, she decided. Still, she couldn't stop herself from asking, "Are the boys all right?"

"They were a minute ago."

Her relief was instantaneous and acute. "Good."

He stared at her, his dark blue eyes probing. "Can I come in?"

"Oh. Of course." Belatedly remembering her manners, she pushed the screen open, and he stepped back to avoid getting hit. "Sorry," she murmured. She was extremely aware of him as he followed her past the entrance to the small bedroom and on into the equally modest living room.

The apartment's diminutive size had seemed cozy to her up until Logan's arrival. Now, with the inclusion of his broad shoulders and long legs, not to mention the rest of him, it seemed cramped. Even so, the sudden uneasy fluttering in her stomach, like a hoard of huge butterflies trying to escape, caught her by surprise. She'd never felt claustrophobic—until now.

Logan hadn't set foot in the apartment since his last housekeeper left. His gaze played over the serviceable oatmeal-colored couch, the upholstered rocker in rusty brown, the single end table and inexpensive lamp, all of which he'd purchased several years ago. Everything looked the same, yet was more inviting somehow, he decided, taking in the moss green afghan, the profusion of pillows in green and cream, and the plants that seemed to be everywhere. With an inner frown, he acknowledged that Gloryanne had put her stamp on the place.

He took in the book that lay open on the small end table, and the way the afghan trailed on the floor. It was an oddly intimate scene, and it made him feel uncomfortable. He walked across to the window to where a makeshift bookcase held a trio of framed photographs, an inexpensive tape deck, scores of paperbacks and more plants. He fingered a fuzzy leaf on one that was similar to the one that was now in his bedroom. "What are these things, anyway?"

"African violets," Gloryanne replied, sitting back down on the rocker and tucking her legs up. Her shorts immediately crept up and with a quick glance at Logan to make sure he wasn't watching, she tugged them back down. "They're sort of sturdy and plain-looking and they don't require much in the way of care. As a matter of fact, they have to be really root-bound before they'll flower, but when they do, they bloom and bloom. They're so pretty then...." Abruptly aware she was babbling, she trailed off, only to have her uneasiness increase when he bent to examine the photographs.

She wondered why she found his scrutiny disturbing. It wasn't as if she didn't know what he was seeing. There was a photo of her as a toddler standing between her parents, the only picture the firemen had been able to salvage after the house fire that had claimed their lives. There was a shot of her with Bev, the two of them wearing party hats as they celebrated her long-awaited eighteenth birthday.

But the photo that seemed to interest Logan was

the largest and by far the most recent, a professional eight-by-ten of the kind routinely taken during the awards ceremony at horse shows. In it, she was sitting atop Je'zhar, decked out in formal English pleasure-riding gear, smiling as she reached down to accept the first place rosette and a big silver platter.

"That's from the All Arabian show at Phoenix last spring," she told him as he studied it. "Je'zhar won the performance class."

Logan eyes didn't waver. "Who's the guy?"

With a sense of shock, she realized she'd forgotten that Jack was also in the picture. "Jack Waylan. The man I used to work for."

Logan frowned. Standing slightly to one side of Glory and Je'zhar, the guy was big and blond and okay-looking, but he was gazing at Gloryanne with a proprietary air that for some reason made Logan's hackles rise.

He set the picture down and turned. "Was he your lover?"

She gave a visible start, and then, as he'd seen her do so often, she collected herself. "I don't think that's any of your business."

He shrugged. "I suppose you're right," he said, telling himself it was her damnable composure that he found so irritating—and not the thought of her in bed with the blond guy. "It sure as hell isn't what I wanted to talk to you about." He walked unhurriedly over to the couch and sat down.

"Just what is it you want to discuss?" she asked pointedly.

He stretched his long legs out, crossing them at the ankles, and leaned back, dwarfing the sofa. "You. And Christopher."

She said nothing, regarding him steadily.

"I want you to stop doing the stuff you're doing," he told her bluntly.

She tensed. "Like what?"

"Like bringing home dogs and baking cupcakes. That sort of stuff."

She bit her lip and appraised him for a moment. He stared back at her unblinkingly, and finally she sighed. "I'll concede that maybe I was out of line with the puppy. I should've discussed it with you first. But the truth is that I saw Fred and just sort of lost my head." She tipped her head to one side, considering. "I'm not sure I understand about the other, though. What possible objection could you have to cupcakes?"

He gave her an exasperated look. "It's not the cupcakes, and you know it. It's all the extra things you've been doing. Like teaching him how to tie his shoelaces and saying you'd make him a Halloween costume." *Like the extra blanket on my bed and doing my chores so I can catch up on my sleep.*

"So what's wrong with that?" she asked carefully.

"I don't want him to start believing he can depend on you," he said flatly, trying to ignore the aggravating thought that maybe the same was true for him. "He's just a little kid, and he doesn't understand that things—and people—aren't always what they seem."

Just the way he put it made her angry. Taking a deep breath, she forced herself to relax, and once she was able to consider what he was saying more calmly, she had to admit she understood his concern. It was even admirable in a way, given that there were a lot of parents in the world who didn't seem to care.

For an instant she considered telling him the truth.

She contemplated revealing to him the circumstances of her own childhood, of explaining that she understood what it was like to be motherless, and that it was *because* she remembered what it was like that she wanted to do all those things for Christopher. Maybe if she explained all that to Logan, he'd see that she would never, ever do anything to hurt the little boy. Maybe then he'd relax and quit worrying so much—and cut her a little slack.

Yet before she could get the words out, he continued. "I also want to know what's going on between you and Josh. It was obvious in the kitchen the other morning that somehow you're finding a way to get around the wall he's built to protect himself. I want to know what you're doing—and why you're bothering. What's in it for you?"

That really did make her mad, but when she finally spoke, her voice was deceptively calm. "You know, I find it interesting that Josh asked me nearly the same thing. As if," she mused, "it's inconceivable that I might like him just for himself. I don't understand why. He's a good kid—both the boys are."

Logan's smile was cynical. "Yeah, that's true, despite the fact that neither of their mothers cared enough to stick around. Maybe that's why your explanation doesn't impress me too much. It's been my experience that when the going gets rough, women take off, and I don't want either Josh or Chris to get hurt because you're feeling some hormonal urge to explore your maternal side."

Glancing down, Glory saw she had a white-knuckle grip on the arms of the rocker. "I see," she said, coming to her feet and pacing away from him. If she didn't put some distance between them, she might actually give in to the almost overwhelming urge she had to smack him. She turned, confronting him across the relative safety of the room. "So what do you want? For them to go through life the way you are? Alone—not trusting anyone unfortunate enough to be born with two X chromosomes?"

His expression hardened. "No, that's not what I want." He picked up the book she'd been reading and rifled meaningfully through the pages. "But I sure as hell don't want them believing that some romantic claptrap called *love* is going to solve all their problems." He put the book down with a decisive slap. "Because we both know it won't."

"Speak for yourself," Gloryanne retorted. Despite what had happened with Jack, she knew that love existed—and not just because she'd read about it in a book, although she didn't discount that for a minute. Romance novels wouldn't be so popular if there weren't a lot of people who knew that love was real and alive—and flourishing. But she'd also witnessed it firsthand, in the tenderness between her parents when they'd been alive.

Logan made a rude sound, bringing her attention back to him. "I suppose you believe in fairy tales and happily-ever-afters, too, don't you, princess?"

No. She knew better than that. What was surprising was that the longer he talked, the more she actually wanted to throw something—at *him*. "What I believe is that you can take a toad out of a pond, but that doesn't make him a prince," she gritted out.

His mouth curled in a sardonic smile. "Cute. But it still doesn't tell me what's going on with you and my nephew."

"It's not anything exactly diabolical. I'm teaching him to ride English."

A split second of surprise showed on his face, before he said, "Well, I want you to stop that, too."

They regarded each other across the narrow length of the room. "And if I say no?" she said softly.

"Don't," he warned, coming to his feet.

She crossed her arms over her chest as he walked toward her, looking for all the world like a man with nothing on his mind more pressing than a little stroll. Except for his eyes. They were hard and shuttered—and inky blue.

"I'm not afraid of you," Glory said when he came to a halt only inches away. As if to prove her words, she stared defiantly up into his hard, handsome face.

"You ought to be," he said silkily. "Because I've had it up to my eyeballs with you."

The eyes in question slid over her plum-colored cotton blouse and khaki shorts, and his expression was so dismissive it cut her to the quick, making her feel suddenly reckless. "You know what your problem is, Bradshaw?"

"What?"

"You've spent too much time around kids and horses—who have to do what you say because you're the boss. But you're not the boss of me, so why don't you take a hike?" Planting her hands on his chest, she gave him a shove, and although it wasn't strong enough to actually move him, it did manage to rock him back on his heels.

His hands shot out and encircled her wrists. "The only thing I'm going to take, princess," he growled, "is this." And with that he hauled her into his arms, his mouth coming down to smother the protest he expected to spring from her lips.

Yet despite all her brave words, it wasn't in Gloryanne to resist him. She surrendered with mortifying speed, just the warm, male, spicy scent of his skin as he pulled her into his embrace enough to steal the starch from her knees. The first incredible, heady taste of his lips had her mouth parting for more, and when his tongue slipped past her teeth and his hands fell away from her wrists, she found herself winding her hands around his neck in a desperate desire to bring him closer.

He delved into her hair, winnowing into the silky mass with the fingers of one hand to tip back her head so he could deepen the angle of the kiss. His other arm encircled her and he began to walk blindly backward, their bodies swaying in rhythm to an age-old song only they could hear. "Yes," Glory murmured. She felt intoxicated by him, the wildness in her blood intensifying madly when he began to blaze a trail of hungry kisses along the sensitive underside of her jaw. "Oh, yes."

And then his legs hit the edge of the couch and they both went down.

Logan was breathing like a bellows. "Dammit, Glory," he said as she began to press a series of soft, open-mouthed kisses up his throat on her way to nuzzling the satiny skin behind his ear, "you're killing me...."

She pressed her face against his neck and smiled, his obvious need lighting her up and exciting her senses like a Roman candle going off. "With any luck at all." He wanted her; and oh, how she wanted him back!

He gave a groan as her teeth closed gently on his earlobe, returning the favor by sliding his hands up the backs of her thighs, pulling her higher on his body, then edging under the hem of her shorts to knead the warm, satiny skin of her backside, making her gasp.

She went to work on the buttons of his black cotton shirt until she could slide her hands inside. The silky texture of the hair on his chest tickled against her palms, and his pectoral muscles felt as hard and smooth as polished bronze.

"Now you," he said hoarsely.

She was so lost in the spiral of sensation winding through her as he rocked her against the proof of his need that for a moment she didn't understand. "What?"

"Your shirt," he repeated, "take it off."

More than willing to do whatever he asked, she sat up, and had already started on the small pearl buttons that ran down the front when her gaze was snagged by a big paper bag that was sitting in the corner. She stared blankly, wondering at the alarm bell that was ringing in her head. After all, it was just the supplies for Christopher's Halloween costume.

The costume Logan had forbidden her to make. That got the attention of her passion-mad brain, as did the thought that came right on its heels—that if Logan had his way, she was to be nothing more to either of the boys than some sort of unofficial hired help. Hadn't he told her right out that he didn't trust women? What was it he'd said? *It's been my experience that when the going gets rough, women take off.* He thought women were mercenary and selfish—

and considerably less trustworthy than a school of sharks.

She suddenly got a terrible sinking feeling in her stomach. Because she knew that even though he wanted her now, once the haze of desire between them cleared, he was bound to come to one of two conclusions. Either that she'd made love with him to try to get her own way, or that she'd never really cared about the boys in the first place. That she had, in fact, only been doing things for them to gain his attention. Which absolutely wasn't true.

But she'd never convince Logan of that. Not Logan, who'd already made it clear he didn't trust her.

And in that instant she knew that no matter how compelling the physical attraction between them was, if she succumbed to it now, she'd only be reinforcing his poor opinion of women in general, and her in particular. Any chance for them to become friends, to have an actual working partnership, for him to ever realize she was worthy of his trust and for her to actually have a home at Columbia Creek, would be incinerated in the wildfire between them, impossible to resurrect.

And she knew she couldn't do it. Because, even though she wasn't sure exactly *why,* she did know she wanted all those things. And that she wanted them far more than a momentary passion, no matter how inviting.

Her brain sent a reluctant message to her hands, first slowing and then stopping the frantic motion of her fingers. She looked down at Logan, her throat tightening with misery despite her newfound resolution.

His skin was flushed, pulled tight across his cheekbones, and his eyes were black with passion. He looked devastatingly handsome and totally appealing, and she found herself praying for the strength to make it through the next few minutes. Not even bothering to refasten her shirt, she took a deep breath and said, "I'm sorry, Logan. I can't do this." And then she scrambled off of him.

Every nerve in his body on the verge of overloading from raw sexual need, Logan was a little slow on the upbeat. "Hey...wait a minute," he rasped, shaking his head as if to clear it. "What the hell is going on?"

Trying to camouflage her shaking hands, Glory hugged her arms to herself and backed away as he surged upright. "I can't do this," she repeated. "It's not right."

He scowled, but he didn't make a move toward her. "Let's not play games, princess," he said after a minute, holding himself very, very still as he regarded her from the couch. His eyes were narrow with censure. "We're both adults. And I want you and you want me."

"Yes," she affirmed shakily. "I do. But not like this."

He clamped his hands down flat on his thighs, as if to stop himself from reaching for her, her open affirmation of need derailing his anger like nothing else could have. Still, his words to her were harsh. "There are names for women who play teasing games," he said to her.

"I know," she murmured miserably. She cleared her throat. "But I wasn't trying to lead you on. It's just that...I can't do what you asked concerning Christopher and Josh. I can't act like I'm nothing

more than an unpaid housekeeper and treat them like
they're some nine-to-five job.'' Her chin came up,
and she met his gaze straight on. ''Because they're
not. Whether you like it or not—whether *I* like it or
not—I already care about them and I can't change
that, even if I wanted to. Which I don't.''

He studied her while he considered her words, his
lids heavy and hooded as he took in her damp, rosy
mouth and the pale red marks that his beard had left
on her tender skin, prompting him to say something
crude but infinitely expressive under his breath.

And then he came to his feet in one smooth flow
of motion, his face wiped clean of all expression, the
only sign he felt anything at all, the suppressed vio-
lence of his hands as he deliberately rebuttoned his
shirt. ''Yeah,'' he said, his voice rough but not angry,
much to her surprise. ''I guess I knew that.'' He tore
his gaze away from her to look down as he stuffed
his shirttail into his jeans with quick, savage movements.

''Logan—''

He looked up and said very softly, ''I'd advise you
to be quiet.''

''But—''

He cut right across her. ''I'm telling you up front,
princess, you give me the slightest excuse and I'm
going to toss you down on the floor and take you the
way we're both aching for. It'll be hot and deep and
hard, and it won't matter that I know you're right,
that I've had my shot at love and marriage and that
I'm done with that part of my life, or that the only
thing we can ever have is some sort of interlude. Say
one more word and I'm going to be inside you so fast
you'll never know what hit you.''

It was obvious he meant it, and she pressed a hand to her mouth to stifle the little sob of desire his words provoked.

Seeing her reaction, his lips twisted in what was meant to be a smile but which came out as more of a grimace. "Smart woman."

And without another word, he walked out, leaving Glory standing there all alone, her emotions in turmoil while her body throbbed from wanting him... and she fought the urge to weep.

It was a battle that she lost.

Glory rested her cheek against the shovel handle and reached up to wipe a trickle of perspiration from her brow. *I must be crazy to spend a Saturday breaking my back this way,* she couldn't help but think.

It'd seemed like such a good idea when she'd awakened full of energy this morning. Ever since she'd first noticed the large weed and grass-choked flower bed skirting one side of the back porch, she'd been imagining what it would look like with a lot of work and a little time.

She could see it clearly in her mind. To the left of the window would go the forsythia, which would be a burst of sunshine during the short, occasionally dark days of early spring, and to the left, at the corner, she envisioned a trio of lilacs, two white and one lavender. Then there would be the bulbs; she already had a score of iris and a dozen daffodils, discovered in a bin at Nielsen's. The next time she went in to Nile, she'd see if Bridget had a seed catalogue and order more.

If she ordered soon enough, the new year would bring crocuses and fragrant hyacinth, and later there'd be tulips, lilies and summer bells. She'd plant pink peonies, and blush-colored pansies, orange and red nasturtiums and marigolds in bronze and gold. The porch trellis would be the perfect backdrop for roses in yellow and crimson and white.

Yes, there was no getting around it, it was definitely a good idea. Or at least, she admitted ruefully, it had been until about twenty minutes ago, which was when she'd first begun to suspect she was getting a hernia. But who would've dreamed the ground would be so hard?

A discreet cough interrupted her musing and drew her eyes to the right, where she found Josh eyeing her curiously, one shoulder propped negligently against the corner support of the porch, his hands shoved into his pockets. "What're you doing?"

"Imagining how all this will look after the work is done," she admitted sheepishly, taking another wipe at her sweaty forehead with a gloved hand. "Is Christopher up yet?"

He shook his head. "Nah. He's still sleeping." He took in the half-cleared garden bed and the rusty old wheelbarrow overflowing with huge clumps of weedy grass, and eyed her small, slim form with new respect. "Have you seen Uncle Logan?"

Boy, had she ever. A little shiver went through her as Josh's innocent question prompted her to remember in graphic, glorious detail just how broad Logan's chest really was. And how firm and silky it'd felt beneath her hands. "He drove over to Quincy," she said, struggling to control the telltale tremor in her voice.

"On a Saturday?" Josh's disbelief was evident.

"But he always stays home on weekends so he can spend time with Chris and me."

Glory felt a pang of guilt. If nothing else, that night in her apartment with Logan had marked the start of an unspoken armistice between them. On the surface at least, in the past week and a half the hostilities between them had ceased, and they were getting along better than she ever would've hoped. *If* you overlooked the small but crucial fact that they were avoiding each other like the plague in a mutual if unspoken agreement to try to extinguish the passion still smoldering between them.

Passion that stubbornly refused to die out, and that, unfortunately, seemed to be growing with every innocent exchange, every accidental touch, every unintended look as they went through the routine of their days. And which, it now appeared, was driving Logan away from the boys, the two people he loved the most.

Glory's sense of guilt increased. "He'll be back this afternoon."

"Good." Josh cleared his throat and shifted somewhat uneasily. "So…you want some help?" he asked in that offhand way Glory had come to know he used as a form of self-protection when the answer really mattered to him.

She straightened. "You mean it?"

He scuffed the toe of one large, disreputable sneaker at the ground. "Sure."

"I'd love it," she said sincerely. "My back's getting tired and my ankle hurts."

He crossed the narrow space separating them and took the shovel from her hands. "Then I'll do this while you go dump the wheelbarrow, okay?"

She stifled a smile, thinking that being dictatorial
must be in the Bradshaw genes. Still, she wasn't about
to refuse when he was offering his help, so she did
as he suggested, stopping on her way back to get a
second shovel out of the garage. They worked together then, laboring in quiet but companionable har-
mony, and in a third of the time it would've taken
Glory alone, the job was done and the ground lay in
rich, loamy clods, ready to be planted.

Josh thrust his shovel into the soil, surveying the
freshly turned earth with open satisfaction, ignoring
the fact that his shirt was wet with perspiration and
his jeans streaked with dirt. "So what're you going
to plant? Vegetables?"

Every inch as dirty and disheveled, Glory shook
her head. "Flowers," she said with quiet satisfaction.
"Enough so I don't have to be stingy with them."

"How do you mean?"

She shrugged. "I knew someone once—" foster
mother number four "—who grew flowers but would
never cut any to bring in the house. I always thought
it was kind of sad—like only baking enough cookies
at Christmas to put out for guests but not enough so
you could eat some yourself." The corners of her
mouth turned up. "All of that work—and none of the
enjoyment. I plan to have enough flowers so that next
year we can have them in every room if we want to."

"You really mean that, don't you?" he said, pulling his T-shirt off to reveal a lean but muscled chest
and shoulders that were already starting to widen. He
began to scrub at his dirty face with the soft cotton.

"You bet. Over there, I'm going to plant—"

"No," he interrupted, his voice muffled. "I mean

about being around next year.'' He lowered the shirt, his gaze clear and direct as it sought hers.

She met it steadily. ''Yes.''

He began to rub at his sweat-dampened hair. ''Did you know this used to be my mom's garden?'' he asked.

Glory shot him a look of astonishment before she could stop herself, but he was still drying his hair and thankfully didn't see it. ''Really?''

''Yeah. Only she grew vegetables.''

She tried to match his casual manner. ''Did your uncle tell you that?''

''No,'' he said, and then proceeded to confound her further. ''She did. When I was younger, she used to come visit and she'd tell me stories about how, when he was a teenager, Uncle 'Gun could never seem to get enough to eat. She said he'd get so hungry he'd steal her carrots and radishes right out of the garden.'' His face creasing in mild surprise, he turned to Glory. ''You know, I'd forgotten about that until just now.''

Glory was still trying to absorb the idea that his mother used to visit. ''Josh,'' she said slowly, ''do you know where your mom is?''

His face darkened, and he got the guarded look so much like Logan's that Glory had come to hate—but miracle of miracles, he didn't shut her out. ''Yeah. Washington, D.C. She's a lawyer. She works as a lobbyist for one of the big conservation groups.'' Despite the fact that he was clearly reluctant to talk about her, Glory thought she detected a faint note of pride in his voice.

''So you hear from her?'' she asked.

''Holidays and my birthday,'' he said sarcastically.

"And every once in a while she calls for no apparent reason at all."

"When was the last time you saw her?"

It was clear enough in his mind that he didn't even have to stop and think about it. "It was right after Christopher was born," he said decisively. "She used to come pretty often before that, but after Uncle Logan and Aunt Melanie got divorced, she stopped. Uncle Logan says she got too busy."

Glory found herself wondering a little at the timing—until she glanced up and saw the raw misery on Josh's face and everything except the need to comfort him flew right out of her head. "Oh, Josh," she said, closing the distance between them to give him a hug. "I'm so sorry. Sometimes adults can be cruel without ever realizing it. If it's any consolation at all, it's her loss."

For the space of a heartbeat, he leaned against her, welcoming her gentle touch, and then he caught himself and pulled back. "Yeah, I guess," he said with forced nonchalance, taking refuge in action by slipping his damp, dirty shirt back on.

Understanding his need for a moment to himself, she began gathering up the gardening tools, piling them into the wheelbarrow.

He gestured toward the garden and went hurriedly on. "If you want," he offered, "I could haul some manure up from the barn in the pickup later this week."

Glory accepted the change in subject with good grace. "That'd be great...if you think your uncle won't mind."

One well-formed brow rose in a gesture remarkably reminiscent of the man in question. "Oh, he'll probably gripe about hauling horse you-know-what in his truck, but it'll be all right. Uncle Logan's more snarl than bite.'' He cocked his head slightly, and the look he turned on her made her feel as if she were the kid and he the adult. "He tries to act tough, but it's mostly a show. You're pretty smart about everything else, how come you haven't figured that out?''

Because just being in the same county with the man addles my brain, she thought with a mixture of humor and despair. Yet Josh's words triggered a memory of something similar Christopher had said, about his dad threatening to spank but never actually doing it, and she found herself envying both boys the rock-solid trust they had in him.

Not that she didn't understand it; Logan loved them fiercely. You only had to see him with them to know how much he cared; his entire manner changed, his dark blue eyes lighting up as if he burned with an inner flame.

It must be wonderful, she found herself thinking, to have him look at you that way, and to know you could count on him for anything and everything.

She straightened abruptly, asking herself what on earth she thought she was doing. For a second there, she'd actually been *pining* for Logan's affection. It must be the heat, she told herself, frantically trying to dismiss the idea that perhaps what she felt for him was more than mere physical desire.

No, she told herself firmly. It wasn't possible. She *refused* to let it be true. She'd simply been out in the sun too long and her brain was a little fried. That's all. But all of a sudden, she needed more than anything to get away from the ranch for a while. ''Didn't you say something at dinner the other night about

there being a swimming hole around here somewhere?'' she asked Josh rather breathlessly.

"Sure," he said, his blue eyes puzzled. "Down by
the river."

She glanced at her watch. "So what do you say we
finish up and take the afternoon off?"

"What do you want to do?"

"Go swimming." A few hours in a nice, cold pond
ought to cool her off—in more ways than one.

"But what about Christopher?"

"It's nearly eleven—even *he* can't sleep forever.
We'll take him with us, of course. By the time we
get everything put away, get cleaned up and changed,
he should be up. We can have lunch, pack a picnic
dinner, and go for the rest of the day."

He hesitated and for a minute she was certain he
was going to refuse. "What about Uncle Logan?"

Now it was her turn to hesitate. "I guess we could
leave him a note," she said reluctantly. There wasn't
a chance on earth he'd take them up on the invitation,
she consoled herself. Not with the way things stood
between them.

Josh gave a careless shrug. "Well...okay. I suppose I have to, anyway." When she looked at him
searchingly, he offered a tentative smile. "You don't
know where it is," he pointed out.

He was such a sweet kid beneath his thorny exte-
rior, she thought, feeling overwhelmed with fondness
for him. Yet she knew better than to press her emotions on him, so she limited herself to an affectionate
smile. "Great." She picked up her shovel and with
great precision balanced it across the wheelbarrow.

"So let's get the lead out, Bradshaw," she told him, starting briskly away, "and move it."

With a wry little face for her sudden energy, he slung his shovel over his shoulder and followed dutifully after her.

Seven

"Watch me, Glory!" Christopher yelled for what had to be the hundredth time, spinning around in a glittering spray of water.

Safely ensconced in a device called a "swim sweater," a spandex tank top with a heavy-duty inner tube sewn into the waist, the youngster bobbed in the space between Glory and Josh, who were floating lazily on a pair of air mattresses.

The pond was actually a part of the river shallows where the ranch met the Columbia River. Separated from the main body of the river by a high, curving spit of rock and sand, the football-field-size depression got enough circulation to keep the water fresh, but was still calm enough that the sun could warm it.

Cut off from the rest of the river, it was also wonderfully private.

"Glory!" Christopher called yet again. "Watch me!"

"Aw, give it a rest, squirt," Josh said. A pair of black, fifties-style sunglasses shading his eyes, he was lying on his back, soaking up the sun. Even though it was coming on to early evening, the temperature still hovered near eighty, rare, although not unheard of, for fall in central Washington.

"Glory likes to watch me," Christopher retorted, paddling over to her and latching onto the end of her air mattress so they were eyeball to eyeball. "Don't you, Glory?"

"You bet," she reassured him. Lying on her stomach, she raised her head to regard him over the pillow of her arms, smiling inwardly when he looked over at Joshua as if to say, *so there!*

He twisted his head back around and sighed, leaning his cool cheek against her warm hand. "I'm glad it's Saturday. It was so hot at school yesterday. Even Mrs. Sandman was grumpy. When I asked her what was the matter, she said she was so hot her panty crows were sticking her." His expression worried, he leaned closer, apparently not wanting Josh to overhear, and whispered, "Do all ladies have panty crows, Glory?"

She choked down the bubble of laughter that tickled her throat, thinking this was exactly what she'd needed. "I think you misunderstood, sweetie," she said, brushing back a strand of his damp golden hair. "I think what your teacher meant was panty hose, which are those skin-colored tights that ladies wear with dresses."

He looked only slightly abashed. "Oh. Like on the TV commercials?"

"Mmm-hmm."

"Ah," he said with sudden comprehension, falling silent for a space of seconds. And then he asked, as he also already had several times before, "Do you think Daddy will come?"

Not if the Lord is feeling compassionate. She didn't want to think about Logan, much less see him. Doing either might force her to stop and think about that ridiculous notion she'd had earlier that he was really beginning to mean something to her, which, she told herself firmly, was entirely farfetched. True, she admired his devotion to the boys and his dedication to the ranch, and she'd be the first to stand up and proclaim that he was a first-class hunk. But it was nothing more than that.

Which doesn't explain, said a persistent little voice in her head, *why just Christopher's innocent mention of his father is enough to cause every muscle in your body to tense, does it?*

Glory swallowed an exasperated groan and closed her eyes, willing herself to relax.

"Well?" the little boy prompted. "Do you think he's gonna come or not?"

"I don't know, Christopher." *I don't know anything—trust me.*

Christopher gave her a little poke. "That's what you said before," he complained.

"And that's what she's going to keep saying as long as you keep asking the same dumb question," Josh interjected.

"I'm not talking to you, Josh," Christopher said tartly, "I'm talking to Glory." He gave her arm an impatient shake. "Are you falling asleep, Glory?"

"Nope." She opened her eyes only to succumb to an unexpected yawn.

He patted her shoulder gently. "It kind of looks like it to me. I think I'm gonna go play with Fred. 'Kay?"

"Sure. There's a towel in the big blue bag. Don't wander off," she admonished him.

"I won't," he said, liberally splashing her with water as he "swam" energetically toward the shore.

"Relax," Josh said. "Christopher knows the rules. He's real good about not taking off."

Even so, Glory turned her air mattress so she could keep an eye on the child, very aware that only a short hike from their campsite the main part of the Columbia stretched nearly a mile wide and who knew how deep.

Josh was correct, however. Once on land, Christopher shimmied out of his safety tube, wrapped himself in a towel and plopped down on the ground to snuggle with Fred.

Logan had been right about that, she thought idly, momentarily forgetting not to think about him. One glance between his son and her dog and it'd been love at first sight, with an entranced Christopher pointing out that Fred looked just like Pluto, his favorite Walt Disney cartoon character.

Her attention on the pair, Glory was only half listening when Joshua said, "Remember the first time you let me ride Je'zhar?"

"Mmm-hmm."

"You said something that's been bugging me ever since."

That got her notice. Her gaze switched to him. "I did?"

He nodded, making lazy little circles in the water with his hand. "You said you'd been in some trouble. And that the lady who taught you to ride helped you out. So what happened? Did you steal a car or rob somebody or something?"

She couldn't see his eyes behind his dark glasses, but she could sense he was watching her, and there was a note in his voice that suggested he'd be impressed if she confessed to being a present-day Ma Barker. Cursing her imprudent tongue while momentarily bemoaning her pledge of honesty, Glory nonetheless told him the truth. "It wasn't anything nearly so exciting. I ran away from the foster home where I was living."

He nearly fell off the raft. "You were in a foster home? How come?" He flipped onto his side so he'd have a clearer view of her, pushing the sunglasses to the top of his head.

She looked across the water at Christopher, who appeared to be using Fred as a pillow. "My parents died," she said softly.

"Oh." He thought about that a minute before he said slowly, "But—I thought…why didn't you go and live with Aunt Melanie's folks?"

She heard the echo of the child she'd been. *Why don't they want me?*

"Raising another child wasn't in their plans."

He stared at her in consternation. "Yeah, but you were family."

"Not everyone is like your uncle." Christopher and Fred switched spots, the child becoming the puppy's cushion and Fred's tail waved so exuberantly it looked like a flag in a high wind. "Like I said. You're pretty lucky to have him."

"Yeah," the boy said. "I guess I am." They floated for a few more minutes. "So where'd you go?"

She sighed, but didn't pretend not to know what he meant. "Portland." It'd been the worst time of her life since her parents had died. "I wouldn't advocate living on the streets to anyone," she told him. "I was there a month and a half, and it was pretty grim." Even so, she could see he was intrigued, making her wonder why horrible experiences always sounded so interesting to the young.

Feeling a pang of concern—the last thing she wanted was for Josh to think that running away was a solution to anything—she forced herself to talk about events she rarely shared with anyone. "I didn't have much money, and I couldn't get a job because I was underage, so it wasn't very long before I had to beg for food and a place to sleep. It was…scary."

"So what happened? How'd you get caught?"

Her voice grew emotionless. "Another runaway I knew was attacked, and all of a sudden I could see that it was just a matter of time before something like that happened to me. So I turned myself in, and child welfare sent me to Bev." She shrugged, rubbing at the goose bumps rising on her arms. Despite the day's warmth, she was feeling a little cold. "The rest, as they say, is history."

On the beach, Christopher tossed a ball to Fred, who appeared to have no idea what was expected of him and was running around in circles. "I think I'll head in," she added quietly. "I'm starting to get chilled."

As she came abreast of him, Josh reached out a hand to detain her. "Glory…" he said awkwardly.

"About some of those things I said that day in the barn about my mom…after what you went through… I guess I must've sounded like a real jerk. It's just that I get so mad sometimes! I mean, what did I ever do to *her* that made her just go off and leave me like that? Not even once, but twice! And why doesn't she even want to know me?"

"You didn't do anything," she said with absolute conviction, forgetting entirely about her own distress and wishing fiercely that she could have just ten minutes alone with the boy's mother to tell the woman exactly what she thought of her. "Whatever the problem is, Josh, it's hers, not yours. Surely your Uncle Logan's told you that."

He hesitated, and she had a sudden, terrible suspicion.

"You have talked to him about how you feel, haven't you?"

His eyes bleak, he shook his head no.

"But, Josh," she said, trying not to sound as incredulous as she felt, "why not? If there's one thing you have to know, it's how much your Uncle Logan loves you. I can understand why the two of you might not have talked about it when you were younger, but surely now…when it bothers you so much…" She trailed off helplessly, and then said more firmly, "You should talk to him."

He gave a dejected shrug. "I've tried, but he gets sort of sad and tense, and then he just seems to clam up." He stopped, cocking his head slightly in puzzlement. "How come you're not like that? Angry, or closed up and stuff?"

"I was," she said simply. "But I got lucky. I went to live with Bev, who had an upbeat philosophy of life, to put it mildly. At first I thought she was a flake, but as I got to know her, I learned she'd had a pretty hard time herself—she'd buried two husbands and her only child. Still, she never let it get her down. She had a bunch of funny sayings that typified her way of thinking, and eventually I guess they rubbed off on me.''

"Like what?" he asked.

Knowing full well he was trying to steer the conversation away from himself, Glory temporarily obliged him. "Oh, she was always saying things like... 'When the train of life gets you down, you've got two choices. You can either throw yourself on the tracks and let it run right over you. Or you can get up, dust off your pants, grab on and go along for the ride.'"

Just as she'd hoped he would, Josh smiled. "I like that," he said thoughtfully. "So what happened? Did she die?"

Glory shook her head, her expression wry. "Not Bev. She broke her hip and had to retire, so she sold her ranch and moved to Arizona. She's too busy terrorizing the retirement community down there to keep a date with her Maker."

"Do you still talk to her sometimes?"

"Sure. We're family now." She hesitated, and then she said quietly, "Bev gave me a lot of things, Josh, but I think the most important one was her belief that sometimes family has as much to do with caring as it does with the blood that flows through your veins."

His forehead puckered as he tried to understand, until finally he said, "Is that supposed to be a nice way of saying I should forget about my mom?" A trace of his former distrust was back in his eyes.

But Glory didn't back down. "No. But don't let *her* failure to be the sort of mother you'd like, have the power to control *your* life. You deserve better—and you have it. Talk to your uncle, Josh."

He sighed. "I'll think about it," he promised.

"Good. And now…are you hungry? Because I sure am." When he nodded, she sent him a cheeky grin. "Let's go, then. I'll race you to shore."

He fell in with her lighter mood with alacrity. "Not a chance." He gave her a mock pitying glance. "You're a girl, and you're…old. I'd pulverize you. It wouldn't be fair."

"Really?" she said in mock amazement, pretending to ponder his statement. "You know, I suppose you're right—*if* I intended to play fair!"

And to his surprise, she reached out and gave him a shove that sent him tumbling off his raft. Laughing at his shout of outrage, which ended abruptly when he went under, she paddled madly for the beach, thinking it wise to be safely out of reach when he surfaced. Her gaze directed back over her shoulder, she was still laughing when she scraped bottom, swung her legs to the ground and dashed out of the water—only to run smack into Logan.

The air whooshed out of her, but it had nothing to do with the impact of their collision and everything to do with finding herself in his arms. "What're you doing here?" she blurted out, the smile vanishing from her face.

Instantly his expression closed, and Glory would've done anything to take back her unthinking words, a desire that only increased when he still managed to say civilly enough, "It's my ranch, princess. I get to go wherever I want."

"I know," she said a little desperately, belatedly aware that in deference to the heat he'd discarded his shirt and was stripped down to nothing more than time-whitened cutoffs and a pair of old Keds. "I'm sorry. I didn't mean that the way it sounded."

To her disbelief, he accepted her apology as easily as that. "Does that mean we can call a truce for tonight?" he asked, looking down into her sun-flushed face as Josh came racing up. "It's been a while since I took any time off to be with these bozos—" he reached out and ruffled Josh's hair "—and I'd sort of like to enjoy it."

Glory couldn't seem to quit staring at him, suddenly aware that in addition to appearing sinfully attractive as usual, he also looked unmistakably tired.

And for some reason, that made everything inside her soften. "Of course," she said, confused by the roller coaster highs and lows of her emotions as she was swept by a great wave of tenderness that was followed swiftly by exhilaration. "I'll give you twenty-four hours, Bradshaw, but then, watch out. The gloves come back off."

His eyes lightened subtly, but before he had time to respond, Josh interrupted them. "Hey, Uncle 'Gun."

"Hey, Josh," Logan responded, directing a brief glance at his nephew.

"You two finished with your little powwow?" the teenager asked.

"It appears so," Logan said softly, his gaze coming back to Glory.

"Good. Then if you'll excuse me?" And before Logan had time to react, Josh scooped Glory right out of his arms and hauled her toward the water, laughing like a banshee when he tossed her in.

It was hard to say who was more stunned. Logan at having his prize stolen away. Or Gloryanne as she arced toward the water. But there was no question who was the first to recover. "That wasn't very polite," Logan told his grinning nephew before Gloryanne had even surfaced.

Still standing at the edge of the water, the boy demurred. "Sure it was. Did you see what she did to me?"

"You think picking on someone smaller is fun?" Logan inquired conversationally. In the background, Gloryanne emerged, sputtering for air, and began to swim for shore, muttering about smart-alecky teenagers with every stroke.

Josh smiled at Logan. "It is when you get away with it," he said cockily, his hands on his hips.

"Oh, really? Then try this." One minute Logan was kicking off his shoes and the next he was across the ground, catching Josh in a flying tackle. While Fred barked and Christopher shouted with glee, they hit the water with the force of a bomb going off, sending a sheet of water spraying over everything.

Shaking her head at such foolishness, Glory waded onto dry land to help Christopher, who was frantically trying to get into his swim sweater so he could join the other two. She barely had the thing over the little boy's head before he was bolting away, yelling, "Hey, Daddy! Look! I can swim! Watch me, watch me!"

Glory couldn't seem to wipe the grin off her face as she toweled the water from her dripping hair.

It was some time later that the three Bradshaw men

emerged, and by then Glory had the food laid out, thankful she'd packed enough to feed a small army, and wondering whether, on some level, she hadn't secretly been hoping that Logan would show up all along.

Yet whatever the reason for their abundant provisions, everyone ate until they couldn't swallow another bite, and when it started to get dark, Logan built a huge bonfire and helped Christopher roast the marshmallows Glory had remembered to pack.

And then, their heads cradled on their arms, they all settled back, the two youngsters sandwiched between the adults, and turned their attention up to the vast black dome of the sky.

The stars glittered like clusters of diamonds high overhead, and for a considerable time all four watched the spectacle above in silent awe until Joshua finally spoke.

"Hey, guess what?" he inquired of the world at large. "I asked Jennifer Sykes to the Harvest dance yesterday."

This announcement was met with a moment of thoughtful silence, until Logan's voice came out of the darkness, as offhand as his nephew's. "Hmm. So what did she say?"

"She said sure," the boy retorted, as if there'd never been a doubt in his mind about her possible reply.

The smile in Logan's voice was impossible to miss. "Well, good. I'm happy for you, Josh."

"Yeah. Me, too."

"Gee, Josh," Christopher said in disgust. "Why do you want to go spend a whole evening with some yucky girl?"

"You'll understand when you get older, squirt," Josh told him. He paused, and then said all in a rush, "The thing is, I sort of volunteered you to chaperon, Uncle 'Gun."

There was another moment of silence at this, until Logan finally said, "Terrific. Just as soon as I get the energy up, I think I'm going to have to kill you, kid."

Josh grinned into the darkness. "Do you think you could wait until after you chaperon?"

Logan gave a resigned sigh, but there was a note of humor underlying it. "Yeah. I guess."

"Look, Daddy!" Christopher interrupted, for once showing an admirable sense of timing. "A shooting star! Oh, this is so cool. Did your dad do neat stuff like this with you when you were a kid, Daddy?"

Logan sighed, but responded amiably, "He sure did, champ."

"What about yours, Glory?"

Fascinated by the entire exchange, Glory smiled. "Yes, Christopher. Both my mom and dad did."

"Even when you were old like Josh?"

Her amusement faded away. She was silent a moment and then she said softly, "No. Not then."

Christopher shifted to look at her, but it was Logan's interest she felt. Even though he hadn't moved, she knew he was listening from the motionless way he was holding himself. "Why not?" Christopher asked.

"Drop it, squirt," Josh said.

Glory laid a hand on the teenager's arm. "It's all right, Josh." To Christopher, she said, "There was an accident, sweetie, and my mom and dad died. That's why."

"Oh. Were you older than me?"

"Yes. I was eleven."

"Does that mean you're an orphan?"

"Christopher!" Josh hissed, and again Glory tried to reassure him, giving him a squeeze with her hand.

"Yes, it does."

"So where'd you go to live?"

"I lived with a lot of different people," she said matter-of-factly, "until I finally went to live with a nice lady who became kind of my second mom."

"When was that? Were you as old as Josh then?"

"Even older," she confirmed.

"How old?" he persisted.

"Seventeen."

"Yeah, that's old," he agreed. He thought a minute and then he twisted around to face Logan. "Daddy?"

Logan's normally dark velvet voice sounded oddly hoarse. "Yes, Christopher?"

"If something happened to you, where would *I* go?"

The little boy didn't sound troubled, merely curious, but even so Logan reached over and pulled him into his arms, holding him tenderly against his chest. "Well, let's see." He pretended to think. "I know. You could go live with my Great-Aunt Jean."

"Is she the lady who sent me those weirdo socks?"

"Those are argyle socks, Chris. Some people think they're fashionable."

Christopher gave a shudder and snuggled closer. "Really," he persisted. "Who'd take care of me?"

"Don't be a dork-face," Josh interrupted before Logan could answer. "Nothing's going to happen. But if it did, I would."

"Oh." Again the child thought for a minute, and then he said, "Daddy?"

"What is it now, Christopher?"

"Could Glory help Josh?"

Logan sighed. "Christopher…"

"Could she, Daddy?"

Glory found she was holding her breath as her eyes met Logan's above the child's burnished head. Even in the questionable light of the fire, there was no mis taking the host of questions she could see in his blue, blue eyes—questions that only time would satisfy.

Logan looked away, turning to gaze pointedly at the sky. "I guess so, son," he said with obvious re luctance. "If she wanted to." There was a definite warning for her in his voice.

The little boy gave a loud, satisfied sigh. "Of course she would. Wouldn't you, Glory?"

"Yes, Christopher," she said, barely overcoming the urge to point out to Logan that if the situation ever arose, he wouldn't be in a position to protest, anyway. "I believe I would."

"Good," the little boy said, as if that settled that. And then the moment was gone as he grabbed Logan by the arm and began to bounce up and down excit edly. "Oh, look! There's a star with colors! And it's moving!"

Josh gave a snort. "That's an airplane, squirt."

"Is not!"

"Is too."

"It is not, Josh! You don't know everything!"

Sheltered by the darkness, Glory listened as the two youngsters' squabbling intensified. Yet despite it, and that last disturbing exchange with Logan, she found she had a faint smile on her face from a contentment that was bone-deep and heart-full. Rome, after all, hadn't been built in a day—and while trust could take a lifetime, it suddenly didn't seem too improbable to think that there might be a place for her here after all.

Logan hushed the boys. "Listen up, you two," he said, and he began to point out the various constellations to them. "See?" he said, pointing north with one big, well-shaped hand, "there's the Big Dipper. It's the one that looks like a gravy ladle and is sort of low in the sky."

Mesmerized by the rich cadence of his voice, Glory shifted, switching her gaze from the stars to him. A shock of night-dark hair tumbled over his brow, softening his powerful masculinity, while the fire glow painted his skin with bold strokes of gold and bronze. He was, she thought almost dispassionately, truly the most beautiful man she'd ever seen.

"...And if you draw an imaginary line up from the two stars that make up the front of the bowl—they're called the Pointers—you'll find the North Star."

"Hey," Josh said, with dawning excitement, "I think I see it."

"Me, too!" Christopher immediately chimed, although he happened to be looking in the opposite direction.

Logan followed his son's gaze and smiled, and believing himself safely concealed by the sheltering darkness, he pressed a kiss of aching tenderness to the top of the little boy's golden head.

And it was then, in a moment of blinding clarity and with a surety she couldn't dismiss, that Glory realized she loved him.

Deeply. Desperately. And completely.

Eight

A storm was moving in. Logan could taste it on the wind.

Even so, as he cut across the far corner of the night-shadowed pasture, he didn't spare a glance at the flotilla of clouds overhead.

Created by shifting strokes of moonlight, great galleons and swift clippers sailed the rising breeze. The night was alive, from the motion in the sky to the rustle of the grass as the wind danced through it, yet Logan barely noticed. His gaze focused inward, he walked furiously, as if he could outpace the emotions rolling through him with the length of his stride.

Something had happened down by the river tonight. Something profound—and disturbing. He'd glanced across the hard patch of ground at Glory and known, without her ever saying a word, that she loved him. Love that he would never—could never—return...because he was all used up inside. First Melanie had shattered his belief in love, and then Annie had destroyed his trust, stripping him of his expectations, until he had nothing left to give a woman. Especially not a woman like Glory, who so clearly deserved more than a down-on-his-luck rancher, who had a ready-made family and no intention of ever opening himself up to heartache again.

It had all come into focus when he'd received that glimpse into her past tonight. Oh, on some level he'd known almost from the first that she wasn't anything like Melanie, that she hadn't been raised as an overindulged child of privilege. She couldn't be, not the way she worked as hard as she did and was always so uncomplaining about doing her share and more. For all her sass and her laughter, there was a strength and a gentleness to Gloryanne that came only from being tested—and persevering.

Still, the reality of her childhood had been a shock, setting off a series of small jolts that had rocked him, rearranging his perceptions. And although he didn't like the way knowing about her background made him feel—as though he wanted to pull her into his arms and shield her against those long-ago hurts—he couldn't help but appreciate the many things it explained.

Like a single, crucial puzzle piece, he now understood not just her need to lay claim to part of Columbia Creek, but also her fierce identification with the boys. And although he still wasn't willing to fully concede that there wasn't any harm in it, he could no longer deny the genuine nature of her affection for them. Which was, he reluctantly realized, the first step on a road that might eventually lead to real trust.

It was a daunting thought. But also a strangely exciting one. Except that it still didn't do anything to answer the question about what to do about that wonderful, frightening look that had been in her eyes—and his own inability to return it.

He could marry her, he supposed, slowly turning the idea over in his mind. It would solve a lot of problems. The boys would get a mother, and Gloryanne would have the home and family she so obviously desired, and even if he couldn't love her, he'd at least get some relief from the unfulfilled desire that seemed to stalk his every waking hour.

But he just couldn't risk it. As things stood right now, when she left she'd be entitled to nothing more than she'd had when she arrived. But if he married her, it'd be just as it had been with Melanie. When things turned sour, Glory would be entitled to half of everything, and he had an obligation to the boys that precluded him from taking any further risks with the ranch.

So where did that leave him? he wondered as he vaulted over the rails of the fence and stepped onto the road that led to the house. If love and marriage were out, what then? A friendship? An affair?

He recalled the look that'd come over Gloryanne's face when he'd suggested they have a truce. She'd appeared by turns startled, then stunned and then shyly pleased, her cheeks turning pink like a little girl who receives an unexpected Valentine. Although he didn't think he'd shown it, that look had made him feel alarmingly tender.

So maybe a friendship wasn't entirely out of the question.

Except that his body had gone crazy at the sight of

her in that tangerine-colored swimsuit. For a significant space of time it had taken all of his control—and the certain knowledge that Josh was watching him like a hawk—not to give in to the temptation to touch her all over. Even now, hours later, thinking about it made more than just his blood pressure rise.

So maybe an affair was the way to go.

He shook his head, feeling as untamed as the wind, and marveled at his own indecision even as he finally admitted that he didn't know what he should do.

And then Gloryanne appeared, emerging to stand on the landing outside her apartment. Rimmed in moonlight, her face turned into the breeze, she looked like a pagan's fantasy, the soft cloth of her shift clinging to her golden skin, her hair a nimbus of honeyed silk billowing around her. He could see the fine blending of her bone and muscle, could sketch with his eyes the deceptively delicate lines that he'd come to know were a foil for a strong and determined spirit.

And suddenly, whether it was right or wrong no longer mattered—just as his reservations no longer signified.

He had to be with her, to hear her satin-soft voice, to share in the warmth of her laughter.

He needed her—if only for tonight.

Glory stared out at the night. From her position on the landing, she could just make out the Columbia to the east, a ribbon of pearl beneath a wind-darkened sky.

The picnic had ended hours ago, with her and Logan saying polite good-nights over Christopher's sleepy head and agreeing to see each other at breakfast, all very mature and civilized.

And the entire time, her heart had been pounding like a drum, beating in time to the revelation that had come to her as clear as a beam of undiluted moonlight.

She loved Logan Bradshaw.

It would have been wonderful if she weren't so terrified.

Deserted by Fred, who'd opted to sleep at the house with the boys, she'd gone through the motions of preparing for bed, showering to rinse the sand from her skin and the smell of the bonfire from her hair, brushing her teeth, changing into the thigh-length ivory chemise she slept in. She'd even turned out the lights and stretched out on the bed.

But she hadn't been able to sleep.

She couldn't seem to turn off her mind, to quit thinking about Logan and wondering what she was going to do, since loving him was both the best thing in her life to ever happen and the worst thing on earth she could do.

On the one hand, she felt a fierce sort of exultation as she marveled at the strength of her feelings for him. She felt desperately alive, connected to the very pulse of life, like one of the great constellations that'd been spinning across the sky earlier tonight.

Yet at the same time she was afraid. Logan had been so desperately hurt in the past, and she didn't have any illusions that simply because she willed it to be so, his disenchantment with women was going to magically vanish. She remembered his words that night in her apartment. *I've had my shot at love and marriage and I'm done with that part of my life.* Winning his trust was going to take patience and determination, and she wasn't certain she had enough of either to see the thing through.

Nor was she quite certain what to do about the desire smoldering between them. Their attraction was mutual and hot, and growing more so with every encounter, but up until this evening she'd been able to delude herself into thinking she could handle it. But loving Logan changed everything. Given the way they were constantly thrown together on the ranch, it was only a matter of time before her need to love him and his desire to have her coincided. And she knew herself well enough to know that, for her, the physical act of love would mean she was trusting him with her heart.

She didn't kid herself. When it came to sexual experience, she was nowhere in Logan's league. If the truth were known, he probably played an entirely different game, kind of like the difference between major league baseball and sandlot softball. And even at that, he'd be a superstar, while the full extent of her repertoire consisted of a few mild teenage flirtations and her disastrous engagement to Jack, for whom she'd never felt anything approaching the kind of overwhelming physical desire that Logan inspired.

Yet she'd been crushed when she overheard Jack tell a friend that her main appeal for him was Je'zhar; that he had big plans for the stallion and so he supposed he could put up with her.

She'd wanted to hide away, to nurse her battered heart in private. But she'd also been angry, an anger that had driven her to confront him. She'd told him right off they were through, but there'd been a lot of heated words exchanged after that, with Glory getting the worst of it when Jack declared that if he'd known at the start she didn't have her uncle's money to back her, he never would have offered for her in the first place—with or without Je'zhar.

The really terrible part was that, in her own way, she'd been as mercenary as Jack. She'd been willing to settle for a man she didn't love for the security of having a home. And still, the virulence of their last exchange had hurt her deeply.

How much worse would it be to face Logan's eventual dismissal? Logan, whom she loved with every fiber of her being, but who'd made it clear that anything that happened between them would only be a temporary affair.

Every instinct toward self-preservation urged her to leave. And yet, if she did, wouldn't she be reinforcing his belief that all women were quitters? She remembered the words he'd said the night they'd nearly made love. *It's been my experience that when the going gets rough, women take off.* Knowing what she did about him, could she live with herself if she did anything that added to his disillusionment?

And how could she leave the kids? Christopher, who was so generous with his love, and Josh, who had actually reached out to her today, forging the first link in a chain of understanding that she needed as much as he did. How could she turn her back on either of them and walk away?

And in addition to their need, what about her own? Who would have thought that in such a short time, she would come to care for both of them so much? But she did; just the thought of not being a part their lives made her shiver with pain. Which was nothing to the agony that ripped through her when she thought about leaving Logan. And yet, the longer she stayed, the harder it would be on all of them if—or was it when?—she finally did leave.

She sighed, turning full-face into the wind that was steadily increasing, trying to calm herself as she looked out over the shadowy yard. The breeze felt cool against her fevered skin, and she welcomed its gentle pressure as it tugged at her hair. The swiftly gathering clouds were beginning to obscure the moon for longer intervals of time, and the swaying shadows made the yard below look unearthly.

And then suddenly, she knew Logan was there.

Like the morning she'd arrived at Columbia Creek, she could feel the weight of his gaze as it touched her, sending tendrils of excitement racing through her veins. And then his tall, solid shape emerged from the shelter of the trees and he began to walk, surely and deliberately, toward the base of the stairs—and her.

He stood looking up at her, unaware of the picture he presented, standing in his boots and a pair of ancient Levi's that hugged his narrow hips and molded his strong thighs. His old jean jacket was open over his hard naked chest, while the wind snatched at the dark silk of his hair.

"Logan..." She thought she whispered his name, but she wasn't certain.

"It's going to be a helluva storm, princess," he said, and she didn't know if he was referring to the weather or the tempest growing between them as he set his boot to the bottom step and began the steep climb up to her.

"Yes," she said softly.

And as simply as that she was in his arms, murmuring soft words of need and hushed exclamations of wonder as she came up on tiptoe to press a lingering kiss to the corner of his mouth.

Around them, the wind surged and sighed, and on some level Glory knew that later she would marvel at the power of the night. But for now, as she twined her arms around Logan's neck, threaded her fingers through the silky softness of his hair and pulled him even closer, all that mattered was the utter rightness of being in his arms.

His mouth met hers as he swung her up into his arms and carried her inside.

Dangerous, Glory thought, but she didn't know if it was Logan she meant or the sweet fire he kindled inside her, or the total rightness of what they were about to share. All she knew, as he set her on the bed and stood looking down at her, moonlight from the window gilding him as the clouds parted for a moment, was that she wanted him—with everything she was and everything she would ever be.

"Are you sure, Gloryanne?" His dark velvet voice was hoarse, the question dredged from deep inside of him.

"Yes." Surprisingly, her own voice was steady as she suddenly knew that whatever else might still be uncertain, this, at least, was unquestionably right. "Are you?"

"Princess, I've never been less certain of anything in my life." He shrugged out of his jacket, exposing even more of his broad, muscled chest with its vee of silky hair arrowing toward his navel. "But short of death, I don't think there's anything that could stop us this time...."

Never had she been more aware of the disparity in their sizes. He was nearly a foot taller than she was and outweighed her by close to a hundred pounds, all of it muscle. In any physical contest between them, he'd win hands down.

And yet, fear was the furthest thing from her mind as she came to her knees, her gaze playing over the sculpted splendor of his body. He had the classic horseman's physique, with wide shoulders tapering to a supple waist, impossibly narrow hips and strong, supple thighs. Just looking at him made her ache. And surprisingly, she found herself reassuring him. "I won't hurt you, Logan," she said, reaching for the hem of her chemise.

He laid his hand on her arm, checking her movement. "Sweetheart, you're making me hurt right now," he said huskily. And before she had time to protest, his hand moved up to smooth the thin cotton of her gown over the thrust of her breast, while the other went around her slender waist to arch her toward him, and his head dipped down, his mouth closing hungrily on the turgid tip. Sensation shot through her and she made a soft little cry of need, her blood turning to liquid fire as he suckled the bead of her nipple and then shaped it with his teeth, setting off explosions of heat deep inside her.

"Logan..." With shaking hands, she felt blindly for the waistband of his jeans, trembling at the heat rolling off his skin. Locking her hands in his belt loops, she tugged with a strength born of desperation and tried to bring him closer.

His head came up, and he murmured a low, deeply masculine sound of reassurance. "Easy," he tried to soothe her.

But she was too caught up in a journey of the heart to play at an ease she was far from feeling. Trying to

slip the metal buttons of his jeans free, she began to
whimper deep in her throat when she couldn't get
them undone because her fingers were too unsteady.
"Please," she beseeched him. "I want to touch you."

"I want to touch you, too," he rasped, reaching
out to trace one long finger down the creamy curve
of her cheek, his hand coming to rest at the base of
her throat, where he could feel her pulse throbbing.
"All over."

His words sent a flush of color through the gold
tones of her skin that he could see even in the dark.
She captured his hand with her own, guided his finger
to her mouth, and kissed it.

His entire body shuddered, and in one lithe move
he stripped off her gown, baring her to his eyes.
"Pretty," he said, his voice a mere ribbon of sound
against the low moan of the wind as his gaze traced
hotly over her, from her high, rounded breasts to the
full curve of her hips, lingering on the tangle of curls
at the apex of her thighs.

"Love me," she whispered, her hands feathering
up his chest, her fingers raking through the surprising
silkiness of the hair there, her thumbs lightly scraping
the dark circles of his nipples, snapping the gossamer
thread that was all that was left of the leash he'd been
keeping on his control.

With a sound that was almost a growl, he tore off
his boots and jeans and came down on the bed like a
man possessed, his mouth engulfing hers in the same
instant that his hard, hot body pressed her into the
mattress, covering her warm, soft curves. He claimed
her hungrily, his tongue nudging against her lips to
sweep inside in a kiss of such shocking intimacy that

Glory gasped, her entire body shivering as wave after wave of pleasure coursed through her.

He broke the kiss, his lips trailing down the line of her jaw, then up to the incredibly sensitive skin behind her ear where he nuzzled her, sending sensation streaking to her breasts and her loins, making her tremble. "I want to be inside you," he murmured roughly. "I want to feel you all tight and hot and wet around me."

"Oh, Logan…" The erotic images had Glory twisting feverishly beneath him. "Yes."

His hands sought hers, his big, rough palms dwarfing hers as he stretched her arms out above her head. "I can't wait," he told her, his chest heaving as he sucked in air, cursing himself for his lack of control.

Their fingers intertwined. "So don't," she said with a shaky laugh, and in the next second the smooth heavy weight of his masculinity nudged the warm, wet core of her desire. He slid solidly home, Gloryanne flexing to meet him like an archer's bow beneath a master's hands. The sensation was overwhelming, and they both cried out.

Gloryanne could feel herself stretching to accommodate him, as she was caught up in a pleasure-pain so intense she couldn't seem to absorb it. She twisted against him, rolling her hips to try and assuage the fever surging through her blood, but each undulation simply seemed to make it more intense, to drive the fire higher, to open her wider and bring him more fully inside her.

She needed to touch him. Sliding her hands out from under his, she lifted her head to press a series of kisses to the base of his throat while her hands traced down the midline of his chest, feeling the flex of muscle and sinew as he rose above her, his hands dropping to cup her hips and pull her even closer.

He began to move. It was like the surge of an ocean tide against the shore—powerful, relentless and wildly beautiful. She could feel herself being flung higher and higher, feel a desperate need to fly even higher, until everything inside her seemed to go still and then explode, and with a startled cry she let go of the last of her restraint and gave herself over to him.

The trust implicit in the gesture shattered something inside Logan. With a low, guttural shout, he surged into her, riding a crest of pleasure so complete that when it was over, long minutes later, all he could do was shudder as he collapsed against her.

Rolling to his side, he wrapped her in his arms.

They didn't speak. As if sensing that words might destroy the languorous glow enfolding them, they lay with their arms locked around each other, Glory's head on Logan's chest, his cheek against her silky hair, and listened to the rising wind as it buffeted the walls around them.

With a rapturous sigh, Gloryanne snuggled closer, and Logan reached over to pull one side of the bedspread over them to keep her from getting chilled. "Thank you...." she said with a satisfied sigh, pressing a sleepy kiss to his collarbone.

He pulled her tighter into his arms. "Shh," he soothed. He didn't want to talk. Not now. Not yet. He felt light-headed, as if his insides had been yanked out, and he wanted to savor the simple pleasure of holding her in his arms for just a little longer.

The time for talk would come soon enough. There was a part of him—that nagging little voice that was turning into such a nuisance—that was already demanding to know what the hell he thought he was doing, besides having just experienced the most fulfilling sexual union of his entire life.

But for now, as her breathing deepened and she lay trustingly in his arms, holding her was all that he wanted—and more than he'd ever thought he'd have.

When Gloryanne awoke sometime later, she was alone on the bed. The wind had risen another notch, and Logan was standing naked at the window, his back to her as he stared out into the fury of the night. Careful not to make a sound, she savored the unfamiliar sense of satiation thrumming through her as her eyes sketched appreciatively over the long, clean line of his spine and she tried to ignore the implication of his hands fisted against the glass.

"You should've told me," he said, without turning.

It didn't strike her as odd that he should somehow sense that she was awake, although strangely enough, even though he still had his back to her, it did make her self-conscious about her own nakedness. Switching on her small bedside light, she looked around for her nightgown. "Told you what?"

There was a pause, and then he did turn, and her eyes widened involuntarily at the blatant evidence of his masculinity. "That you'd never been with a man before."

She tried hard not to stare, but found she couldn't help herself. He was so different from her. So very male. Part of her was embarrassed that she couldn't seem to stop looking at him, but there was another part—a part he'd created with his loving—that longed to explore his foreign nudity. "Who says I haven't?" she said distractedly.

A faint smile turned up one corner of his mouth. "Let's just say I could tell. And even if I couldn't, all it'd take to clue me in is the look on your face right now—like you can't decide whether to tackle me or run like hell."

Her cheeks warmed, and with a sense of relief, she spied her gown on the floor. "I still don't think it matters," she murmured, reaching for the chemise and turning it right side out. She pulled it over her head, tugging it into place.

The bed dipped under his weight. He cupped her chin in one big hand, his thumb grazing her lips. "You should've told me," he repeated.

Despite the tether of his fingers, her chin came up. "I don't recall asking you the details of your... intimate past. I didn't think you needed to hear about mine."

"Princess," he said dryly, "you didn't *have* a past up until a few hours ago." The look he sent her was a rebuke in itself, and then his voice dropped, gruff with concern. "My blood was running pretty hot. You're not very big—and I am. Did I hurt you?"

In spite of the intimacy they'd just shared, for a second she was mortified by his calm acknowledgment of his own attributes; he didn't have to sound so...complacent about it. And then the memory flashed through her of that first moment of his possession, the sense of incredible fullness and of being pierced clear to her soul, and a soft, secret smile touched the edges of her mouth. "No," she said huskily. "It was more wonderful than I ever imagined." *Because it was you.*

He was staring at her, a muscle in his jaw twitching as if she'd struck him rather than smiled. "I'm beginning to wonder what else I don't know about you," he said slowly.

"Well don't." She turned her head slightly, freeing herself of his gentle hold on her chin. "I'm not trying to hide anything, I promise you." She clasped his fingers in her own and, as she had before, pressed his palm to her lips for a tender kiss. The result was immediate and intensely gratifying as a tremor rolled through him—until he snatched back his hand and stood.

"We need to talk," he said brusquely, pacing restlessly back to the window.

"Actually, we don't," Gloryanne said calmly. At some point during the past few hours, all of the fears she'd entertained over the course of the day had disappeared, replaced by the certainty that he needed her love. She'd never known anyone who needed it more, and even though she didn't have any illusions that it would be easy, she intended to see it through. Wasn't she always telling Logan she was tough?

He turned to stare at her in disbelief. "What's that supposed to mean?"

She shook her head at his agitation, the strength of her feelings for him lighting her up like candle glow. "Logan, I lost my virginity—I didn't have a lobotomy. I assume you're about to tell me that even though we just shared this incredible experience where the earth moved and time stood still, it doesn't mean we have to get married—or something like that. But you see," she said gently, "I already know that. So why don't we just agree to take things as they come? To give it some time and see what happens?"

For the space of several long, drawn-out moments, her eminently practical suggestion was met by crushing silence. Until he finally said, in a seemingly incredible leap of logic, "There's a payment coming due on the ranch in three weeks. It's for twenty-five thousand dollars—and I don't have it."

But Glory understood perfectly, and was so overcome at the trust he was according her that it took her a second to get control of her voice. "How short are you?" she said finally.

His tone was brittle and self-mocking. "Oh, about seventeen thousand plus change."

"Hmm." She considered it. "I have about twenty-five hundred in the bank," she mused idly. She looked up at him apologetically. "The rest went to get me out of my contract with Jack."

His gaze sharpened on her. "Why?"

"Why what?"

"Why did you need to do that?"

She shifted uncomfortably. "We were engaged—until I found out he was more interested in Je'zhar than me." She shrugged. "I couldn't stay after that." She ignored the odd look he was giving her, and went on hurriedly, "What about if we sell the Cherokee? With my savings, the Jeep and my trailer, we should have enough. It'd be close, anyway."

For an instant his eyes warmed with something that looked suspiciously like appreciation, and then he shook his head, rejecting the idea out of hand. "I don't think so."

Of course not, she thought, trying to ignore the sharp sting of rejection that he wouldn't accept her help. And yet she thought she understood; without the Jeep it wouldn't be as easy for her to leave, which he obviously still believed was only a matter of time. But now was hardly the time to start feeling sorry for herself, she reminded herself, forcing her mind back to the issue at hand.

Yet when another possible solution to the problem suggested itself, she hesitated, afraid he might misunderstand it, as well. She looked over at him uncertainly. "I'm sure you've already thought about this, and that there are a million reasons I know nothing about which explain why it would never work, but…what about selling off a portion of the orchards?"

"No," he said, almost before the words were out of her mouth. "Bradshaws have always raised apples at Columbia Creek."

"But you don't," she said, feeling her way carefully. "You raise horses."

"You don't understand…" he began, only to trail off as his gaze turned inward.

"What don't I understand?"

He shrugged. "You would've had to have known my dad," he said slowly. "He was an orchardist right down to his fingertips, and he'd have sold my sister or me before he'd have parted with a single one of his trees, much less an entire block of them."

"But you're not your father," she pointed out softly.

For a considerable space of time, he stood as still and unreachable as a statue, as if considering her statement. But all he eventually said was, "I'll think about it." And although some of the terrible tension that had driven him to the window began to disappear, he still didn't make a move toward her. "There's an aspect of it you may not have considered."

"And what's that?"

"That over the long term we'd probably be taking a loss. That means," he said flatly, "less money in both our pockets." His eyes were dark—and as impenetrable as the storm-tossed sky outside the window.

She heard the question in his voice, then, and knew a moment of stark despair as she wondered if he'd ever understand that it wasn't the ranch's potential cash value that mattered to her, but its incalculable worth as a home. With Christopher and Josh, Logan had created a family here—and to her, that was worth more than if the fields were planted in gold.

But she didn't try to tell him that. Because it was a matter of trust. And trust, like proving your worth, was one of those things you couldn't force, and either Logan would come to see her clearly—or he wouldn't.

But there was nothing she could do about it tonight. Nor did she intend to try. Seeing him standing there, his body tall and lithe and bronzed, had been doing strange things to her heart rate for some time, and they'd spent enough time on talk. Tonight was for loving—not for repining over the past or worrying about the future.

So all she said was "That's all right. Money has never been my weakness." And then her voice dropped, growing low and unintentionally seductive. "Aren't you getting cold?"

Even in the dim light she could see his body tighten in response to her hopeful tone.

"You are—hands down—the damnedest woman I've ever known." With a bemused shake of his head, he padded unhurriedly back to the bed, where he stood looking down at her.

"Thanks," she murmured, trapped in the mysterious depths of his eyes.

"Take off your gown." The words were no more than a whisper of sound, yet they sent ripples of excitement spreading through her. With shaking fingers she did as he asked, unable to tear her gaze from the heated passion growing steadily on his face as he took it from her and dropped it deliberately to the floor.

And then, although still refusing to hurry, he lowered himself to the bed and was rewarded for his patience as she melted bonelessly into the hard curve of his body, the blood already singing through her veins even before his lips began a slow slide down her body.

She whimpered, her hands feverishly tracing the line of his broad shoulders and the sculpted strength of his arms, and he made a low sound of satisfaction. "Did you really mean it about the earth moving?" he asked.

"It was a ten on the Richter scale," she affirmed breathlessly, coming up off the bed as his lips closed over one tender nipple.

And then he was fusing them together, setting a rhythm that was hot and hard and hungry, and she was crying out, her voice rising to blend with the keening wind at the incredible fulfillment of having him inside her as she was claimed by the first in a series of shattering climaxes.

And still, with a need born of desire but sustained by love, she continued to meet him, touch for touch, thrust for thrust, until his voice joined hers to become one, and they were caught by the power and the beauty of the passion storm between them.

They were so intent on each other that they never even noticed the lesser storm breaking harmlessly beyond the window.

Nine

"Uncle Logan?"

Looking up from the account ledger he was going over one last time, Logan glanced from Josh to his watch, frowning as he saw that it was nearly midnight. "Last I heard, Monday's still a school day," he said mildly. "Shouldn't you be in bed?"

His nephew gestured at his pajama bottoms. "I tried, but I can't sleep. Do you think we could talk for a minute?"

Logan set his work aside. "Sure." Although he was operating on very little sleep, when he'd finally awakened this morning—in his own bed, after reluctantly leaving Glory sometime before dawn—he'd felt as if a weight had been lifted from his shoulders.

It had taken him a while to figure out what was going on, and then he'd realized that he'd come to a decision about Glory's suggestion that they sell off some land.

He shook his head in disbelief, still feeling slightly bemused. Here he'd been, driving myself into the ground trying to hold things together, and all the while the solution to his financial problem had been staring him right in the face. His leaseholder, Cal Welmar, had been after him off and on for years to sell a portion of the orchard that bordered Welmar's land, but Logan had never even considered it. Why? Out of habit—and because it wasn't what his father would have done.

But as Glory had pointed out, he wasn't his father. Hell, he loved the land, but one of the first things he'd done when he inherited the ranch was to arrange for Cal to take over Columbia Creek's fruit-growing operation. There was so much specialization these days, such a demand for certain varieties, that there was no way to compete if you weren't willing to give it your all. And he wasn't. From the time he'd been Christopher's age, it had been the horses that had interested him.

So he'd called Cal first thing this morning, and the orchardist had leaped at an opportunity to discuss a possible sale; it had been all Logan could do to hold the man off until tomorrow.

Yet he had, because for the first time in months he'd wanted some time just for himself. He'd done the bare requirement of chores, and then he'd taken the rest of the day off, spending the afternoon taking Glory and the boys sight-seeing, showing them Wanapum Dam, and the towering steel horses sculptor David Govedare had erected high on the hill above Vantage, and the stone trees at Ginkgo Petrified Forest, and ending the day with a leisurely dinner in Ellensburg. It was one of the most pleasant times he'd spent in years, and he'd enjoyed every minute of it.

The only dark note had been struck by Josh, who'd been quiet and strangely withdrawn most of the day. Logan had chalked it up to teenage moodiness, but now, as he studied the boy, he could read the strain on his nephew's smooth young face. Ignoring a faint sense of alarm, he said evenly, "What's up? Already worrying about the dance next weekend?"

"No." Josh crossed the kitchen to perch on the chair opposite his uncle's, his expression grave. "I need—that is, I want to ask you something about my mom."

Logan's fingers tightened on his pencil, but his mild expression didn't change. "Okay."

Josh averted his gaze, picking at a red thread that had somehow attached itself to the dark blue cotton knit of his pajama pants. "I just wanted to hear why she gave me to you."

Logan sighed. "I've told you, Josh."

"Yeah, I know. But I want to hear it again."

"There's nothing new. She went away to college and fell in love, but when she found out she was expecting you, she realized she was too young to get married. It was close to graduation and she had an offer to work in Washington, D.C. One that would give her an income while she went to night school and studied law."

Logan rattled off the information, struggling to temper his impatience with the fact that this was information they'd been over a hundred times. "Your mom is ambitious. She wanted more than to be the wife of a farmer. Not that there's anything wrong with

that, but it just wasn't for her. Still, she wanted to
have you—and I wanted to raise you. So everything
worked out.''

Josh sent him a quick, unfathomable look, and he
found himself adding almost defensively, ''She was
awfully young, Josh.''

''She was older than you.''

''Yes, I know, but...people mature at different
rates. Maybe I was young chronologically, but by the
time you came along, I'd been running the ranch by
myself for a year since your grandpa died, and I was
ready to be a father.''

He'd always felt centered here, his heart tied to the
silver gray sweep of the Columbia and the broad plateaus stretching endlessly toward the horizon. Even
as young as he'd been, he'd had a sense of belonging
that his sister had never shared, and it had given him
the inner stability necessary to raising a child.

Annie, on the other hand, had always been dissat-
isfied with the vast expanse of central Washington,
calling it ''the great wasteland.'' From an early age
she'd yearned for the hustle and excitement of big
city living, impatient to make her mark in what she'd
called the ''real'' world. She'd looked at Josh and
seen only liabilities; he'd looked at Josh and seen the
possibilities.

''I wanted you,'' he said yet again, at a loss to
explain his sister's decision when he'd never fully
understood it himself.

Josh peered at the thread decorating his pajamas.
''But...why did she stop coming to see us?''

Logan's blue eyes darkened as he recalled his sister's last visit, and he began to tap the pencil against
the account book, unconsciously seeking an outlet for

the disquiet the memory caused him. ''Your mom was busy getting her career off the ground, I had my hands full with you and Christopher, and it was hard to find a good time for all of us to get together,'' he said, giving the boy the usual, edited version of the truth. ''I guess we both stopped trying.''

The argument that had led to their estrangement had begun innocuously enough, beginning just as Annie had been preparing to leave following a three-day visit. After loading her bags into her rental car, Logan had finally managed to get a fussy three-week-old Christopher down for a nap, when Josh, agitated as he always was when the time came for one of his mother's departures, had gone in and deliberately awakened the baby by giving him a painful pinch.

Logan had understood that Josh was looking for attention and reassurance, but he'd also known that the best way to give it was by behaving as he always did, and so he'd reacted accordingly. After a firm set down, he'd sent his nephew up to his room to reflect on what he'd done.

The minute the boy had disappeared up the stairs, Annie had turned on him. ''Don't you think that was a little harsh?'' she'd demanded, her own opinion obvious.

''No,'' he'd said simply.

Her lips had pursed with disapproval. ''Well, I do. Maybe you're just too tired to see it,'' she'd added in what he could remember thinking had to be the understatement of the century. Hell, he'd been exhausted, what with her ''surprise'' visit, and from trying to run the ranch while single-handedly taking care of both an infant and an active eight-year-old. ''He's very bright,'' she'd gone on, ''and a little high spirits at this age is to be expected. Besides, it's natural for him to be jealous of the baby."

Logan had been quite aware of that, but he'd also known that for all their sakes, he couldn't allow Josh to take out his frustrations on Christopher, and he'd resented his sister's criticism. Particularly when it never seemed to occur to her that *she,* not Christopher, was the cause of most of her son's current frustration and distress.

As if it had happened yesterday, he had a clear picture of the scene in his head. In contrast to his messy kitchen and his rumpled self, Annie had looked elegant and untouchable in her designer suit. "Perhaps," she'd said coolly, "Joshua should come live with me for a while, until you're more up to coping." Her casual suggestion had paralyzed him. Granted, he hadn't been in the best emotional shape, what with Melanie's recent desertion and his divorce becoming final days after Christopher's birth. But that had only made the threat implicit in her words seem even worse.

How could she believe, even for a second, that he'd willingly give up the little boy he'd raised since birth? The child, who if not precisely a child of his blood, was most certainly the son of his heart?

And how could she look at him so calmly and make a suggestion that reduced that child to an inconvenience to be passed off to someone else when things got a little rough?

To this day, Logan could remember the fury that had roared through him—fury fueled by pure, unadulterated terror—that she might actually mean to take Josh away. Just the thought when he'd already lost so much had been intolerable, and he'd struck back, determined to demolish the idea before it ever had a chance to get established in her head.

"Josh is mine, Annie," he'd said forcefully. "*Period.* You lost your rights the day you gave him over into my care."

His sister had flushed a little. "But I'm his mother."

As if he needed the reminder. It was the very strength of her claim that had been so threatening. "Any woman who'd turn her back on her child the way you did forfeits her right to the name," he'd said coldly.

Annie had always had a temper, and his scathing words had set it off. Her eyes, as blue as his own, had narrowed ominously. "I'm his mother," she'd repeated stubbornly, "and you'd do well to remember it, little brother. If I want him with me, that's my choice."

Without a word, he'd gone into his bedroom and tucked Christopher back into bed, carefully shutting the door behind him before he'd come back into the kitchen where she still stood.

He'd faced her then, and there'd been a distance separating them that had been infinitely bigger than the space of the kitchen.

In Logan's mind there had been a sense of betrayal so vast he'd barely been able to fathom it, and from it had sprung the determination to do whatever it took to keep Josh with him. "I'd advise you to think about it, Annie," he'd said. "Because I'm warning you— I'll fight you every inch of the way and with everything I've got. We both know how image-conscious your political friends can be. How effective a lobbyist do you think you'll be if everyone's watching you—

and wondering what kind of woman abandons her own child?''

She'd paled, and inwardly he'd died a thousand little deaths at the pain in her eyes at his attack, but his resolve hadn't wavered.

It hadn't taken her long to rally, anyway. ''I know you, Logan. I practically raised you after Mama died. You wouldn't do that. It's not in you to be cruel.''

''Try me,'' he'd said in a deadly quiet voice. ''For eight years I've kept my mouth shut and let you waltz in and out of my and Josh's life whenever you got the urge. And while you were off drinking martinis at some swank political function, I've been the one who's comforted 'your' son when he cried for days after you left, and I've been the one who's had to answer his questions when he's asked why he doesn't live with his mother like other kids do.

''Well, I've had it, *big sister*. As far as I'm concerned, you can take your superior air and your designer luggage and get the hell off my ranch—and away from both my kids—and not come back until you're invited.''

She'd given him a long, incredulous look, which he'd met without blinking, and then with an angry little cry she'd snatched up her purse and stormed toward the door. ''Don't hold your breath waiting for me to show up, Logan,'' she'd warned. ''Because I won't be back!''

And she'd meant it. Oh, they'd spoken regularly on the phone since then; polite, inane conversations. But she'd never again mentioned Josh coming to live with her, and when Logan had finally swallowed his anger and his fear—and his pride—and extended an invitation to her to visit, she'd declined, claiming the timing was inconvenient.

And so it had gone for the past six years. Sometimes, in the middle of the night, he found himself worrying that Josh would blame him for driving his mother away, and he regretted his harsh words. Yet it had been his sister's choice to stay away.

Which only went to show how little Josh really meant to her, he always reminded himself. It would take a hell of a lot more than a few sharp words to keep *him* away from either of his boys.

He realized Josh was watching him, the boy's expression questioning the play of emotion that must be coloring his face, and he struggled for composure. "It's late," he said quietly. "And there's really nothing more to say."

Josh's jaw jutted stubbornly. "You always say that, Uncle 'Gun. Maybe," he said, watching his uncle carefully as if to gauge his reaction, "maybe I should talk to my mother."

Logan refused to rise to the bait. "Maybe you should—except that I don't know how to get a hold of her since she hasn't sent us her new address since her last promotion. We'll hear from her at Thanksgiving, which isn't that far away. I think," he added coolly, "that this will keep until then, anyway."

"I knew you'd just put me off!" Josh said angrily. "And that's exactly what I told Glory, only she didn't believe me!"

Logan went very still. "You discussed this with her?"

Josh's chin rose defiantly. "Yeah, I did."

"I see. And what did she say?"

"She said I should talk to you. Although I don't

see why! You don't care anyway!'' With typical teen-age dramatic flair, he stood up so abruptly his chair toppled over. ''It wasn't *your* mother who abandoned you!''

Despite Josh's agitation, Logan had relaxed infin-itesimally with the reassurance that Glory hadn't tried to undercut him. It gave him the ease to see the hurt underlying the boy's embittered words, but still he felt that the best thing he could do for now was to say nothing. He needed time to think, time to consider how much he could tell Josh without hurting the teen-ager's sensibilities even more.

''Go to bed, Josh. It's late, and we're both tired.'' He dropped his gaze to the ledger. ''We'll talk about it another time.''

''Dammit, Uncle Logan—''

Although he didn't raise it, this time there was steel in Logan's voice. ''Go to bed.''

With a sharp curse, the teenager spun on his heel and stormed out of the room.

Glory guided Je'zhar down a narrow track that cut through one of the orchards. The stallion was jumpier than a pogo stick, shying at every little noise and shadow, but Glory barely noticed. She was too busy trying to wrestle her unruly feelings into order.

It wasn't easy. The night she and Logan had spent together had been everything she'd ever dreamed the passion between a man and a woman should be. And although she'd meant what she said about taking things as they come, their relationship had been re-markably amicable the past few days and she was finding it increasingly difficult not to harbor hopes for the future.

Yet despite his obvious desire for her, Logan
hadn't done anything to indicate that he'd had a
change of heart about love or commitment. *All we
can ever have is some sort of interlude,* he'd said that
first night in her apartment; she had no reason to believe he felt any differently now. And she, better than
anyone, knew you couldn't make someone want you.
All those years of being shuffled from one foster
home to another had taught her that.

Or at least, they should have. Yet in one small corner of her mind—and the better part of her wayward
heart—she couldn't help but hope that Logan might
come to see that she belonged with him and the boys
at Columbia Creek. Even if the more pragmatic part
of her kept warning there was about as much chance
of that as of a blizzard in July. Not totally impossible.
Just not very probable.

She sighed and guided Je'zhar out of the trees onto
a trail that zigzagged steeply up the side of one of the
sage-dotted hills, smiling when the stallion snorted
back as if in answer. "What's the matter, fellow?"
she asked him fondly. "That chestnut filly still giving
you the cold shoulder?"

He gave a disdainful toss of his head and tugged
on the bit, as if to express his opinion that a good
hard run would make them both feel better.

Glory's smile widened slightly. "You're right."
And as quickly as that, she gave Je'zhar his head.
They cleared the crest of the hill in a single bound as
the stallion launched into a ground-eating canter.
Heaven would be like this, Glory thought as they flew
across the ridge and she was swept away by the sensation that was like no other. *All golden light and*

sweet-smelling air and a blooded horse flying into the sun...

It wasn't until she started to rein in that she heard the unmistakable sound of another horse. Slowing Je'zhar to a walk, she twisted in the saddle, feeling a distinct thrill as she saw it was Logan on the big dun gelding approaching at a lope. "Hi," she called happily as Je'zhar pranced beneath her. "You got done early—"

"I'm starting to think you have all the brains of a fruit fly!" he snapped, reining in so quickly the dun practically stood on its head. "What do you think you're doing up here all by yourself?"

Je'zhar's small, pointed ears flicked uneasily toward his terse voice, while Glory's hands tightened involuntarily on the reins as she shot him an incredulous look. "Tap dancing, Mr. Bradshaw. Can't you tell?" The stallion sidled sideways and she nudged him with her heels, urging him forward—pointedly away from Logan.

There was a moment of charged silence before Logan gave an exasperated sigh and spurred his long-legged gelding after her Arabian. "Look... I didn't mean to take your head off," he said gruffly. "It's just that the last time you took off by yourself, you racked up your leg, okay?" His gaze slid knowledgeably over Je'zhar, taking in the athletic bounce to the horse's step, undiminished despite the stallion's recent run. "With this guy, you'd be lucky not to break your neck."

For a second, Glory was so startled by his admission that he'd come after her out of concern, she nearly fell off her horse. "I'm sorry," she said, her surprise evident in her voice. "It didn't occur to me that you'd worry."

He flushed as if he'd been caught doing something wrong. "Just try to be a little more careful," he growled, avoiding her gaze by looking out at the eastern horizon.

"Sure." The seconds stretched into minutes. When it became clear he wasn't going to say anything more, Glory found herself sneaking more and more peeks at him while she wondered what was going on behind that leanly handsome face. "So…" she finally ventured. "Did you come up here just to yell at me? Or was there something you wanted to discuss?"

His gaze jerked to her, and then a faint smile tugged at the corners of his lips and his posture relaxed. "Anyone ever mention you've got more nerve than a high-wire act in a windstorm, princess?"

She smiled back. "Nobody but you, cowboy. I guess you just bring out the daredevil in me."

Their eyes met, and suddenly the moment was fraught with electricity as the memory of their lovemaking seemed to sizzle in the air between them. For the life of her, Glory couldn't seem to tear her gaze from him as her mind was flooded with images of the two of them entwined, the velvet weight of his mouth plumbing hers, his slightly callused hands gently shaping her breasts, the hair-roughened columns of his thighs brushing hers.…

It was Logan who finally found the fortitude to look away—but not until a bright blue flame of desire had ignited in his eyes. His gaze pointedly averted, he cleared his throat. "I had a call from Welmar this afternoon. He's made a firm offer on the south orchard."

Glory dragged a breath into her lungs, and actually had a split second where she couldn't remember who Welmar was. "And?" she said, frantically thinking until she recalled he was the orchardist Logan had mentioned might be interested in buying part of the land.

He shrugged, but there   a lightness to the movement that was revealing   d it's a fair offer, with a sizable chunk of cash for the down that would more than handle the payment we have coming due."

His use of "we" was like music to her ears. "Then do what you think is best," she told him, pleased that she sounded as composed as he did. "If you're comfortable with selling, go ahead. And if you're not, we'll find another way." She didn't have a doubt that Logan would do what was best for the ranch.

He gave her a long, shuttered look. "You're sure?"

"Yes."

He shook his head as if he couldn't believe her ready compliance. "Okay then."

They again fell silent, riding steadily along until Glory shifted in the saddle and gestured with her free arm toward the sweep of terrain stretching to the east. "It's sure pretty," she offered.

Below them, the land rolled in variations of beige, ocher, sandstone and brown down to the broad Columbia; a slight evening haze was beginning to settle over the river, cloaking it in a silvery mantle that shimmered where it touched the pale azure sky, while to the south the orchards marched up and down the waving hills, each row of trees lined up precisely, their leaves a quilt of green.

He, too, drank in the scene, his eyes lighting with appreciation. He said slowly, "You really think so?"

She gave him a brief look, perplexed at the thread of disbelief running through his voice. "I don't see how anyone couldn't."

His gaze locked on the far horizon, he said quietly, "My sister Annie didn't. All she saw was dirt and sage and bunchgrass."

Glory didn't have the slightest idea what was going on behind the intense indigo of his eyes, but she wasn't about to let the opportunity he was giving her to satisfy some of her curiosity slip by. She hesitated, uncertain where best to start, then said softly, "You both grew up here?"

For an instant he looked startled, as if it surprised him that she didn't know more about his past, and then he said neutrally, "Yeah. There's been a Bradshaw here for nearly a hundred years. My paternal grandfather filed his claim at the turn of the century, and my dad would probably still be going strong if he hadn't been killed in a tractor accident."

He fell silent, and Glory prompted gently, "When was that?"

For a minute it seemed as if he might not answer, and then he gave a little shrug. "The summer after I graduated from high school. That's when I took over running the ranch."

"And your mother?" Once out of the barn, Gloryanne couldn't seem to get her galloping inquisitiveness recorralled.

He shrugged. "I don't remember her. She died when I was four."

"And Annie?"

"What about her?"

"Where was she when you lost your dad?"

"Away at school. She had a scholarship to Washington State."

"Were the two of you close?"

"When we were younger, I guess. She's only a few years older than I am, and we sort of raised each other." Logan's expression grew distant as he remembered. "Dad was always absorbed with the orchards, so we were left to our own devices pretty much." He made a gesture that encompassed the steppes around them, scorched to a pale brown after the long summer's heat. "Believe it or not, we used to come up here to play, cops and robbers, cowboys and Indians, that sort of thing. She'd be the good guy and I'd be the bad. Kid stuff... Sometimes it's hard to believe I was ever that young."

He was a lot like the river, Glory realized. Contained on the surface, while underneath swirled deep and powerful currents of emotion....

It was an observation that seemed even more appropriate when he murmured obliquely, "And even then, Annie always had to win."

She thought it a curious thing to say, but some instinct warned her not to comment, so she said instead, "How old were you when she left Josh with you?"

"Nineteen."

So young! "And how old was Josh?"

"Less than a month."

She stared at him in stunned respect, trying to imagine how it must have been for him, all alone at Columbia Creek with an infant to raise. He would have been on the brink of manhood, a difficult time all by itself even without being saddled with such a huge responsibility. "Wasn't that awfully young to take on raising a child by yourself?"

He turned to give her a long, level look. "You sound just like Josh." He looked away for an instant, and when he looked back, it was as if he'd reached some sort of decision. "Listen, princess, I know Josh's been talking to you, and that right now he's got a romantic notion that there's some great mystery behind his mother's lack of interest in him. But the truth is, motherhood simply never interested Annie. On a scale of one to ten, Josh ranked right around minus eleven."

Given her aunt and uncle's rejection, it was an attitude Glory was painfully familiar with—but she could also sympathize with Josh's curiosity. "I understand," she said softly, "but I think perhaps Josh needs the chance to discover it for himself."

Logan's face turned stony, and suddenly that closed look that meant she'd overstepped her bounds shadowed his face. "He's had enough rejection in his life."

"He's not a child anymore, Logan. He's becoming a young man, and you can't protect him forever."

He shrugged. "Maybe. Maybe not. But it's not your concern—and it *is* mine." There was no mistaking the finality in his voice.

Seconds later, the first of the night birds began to sing, the sound rising and falling in a pattern that all of its species made, and despite Logan's dismissal, Gloryanne's optimism refused to be dimmed, pointing out that at least he'd spoken to her, instead of shutting her out as he had before. Still, she couldn't help but think rather wistfully how easy it would be to be a bird, with none of the thousands of choices that humans were forced to make.

Logan reached down to smooth a tangle out of the dun's black mane. "There was something else I wanted to ask you, anyway," he said, unexpectedly breaching the silence. "I was wondering," despite the casual tone there was a foreign note of formality in his voice, "whether you'd like to go to the dance with me Saturday night."

"Really?" she said, unwilling to admit even to herself how much she'd been hoping he'd invite her. "You don't have to ask just because you…I mean, because we…" For some reason, her consternation seemed to ease him. He smiled, revealing a groove at one side of his mouth that in a less intimidating man might have been called a dimple. "Yeah," he said with disarming frankness, slanting her a slow, heavy-lidded look. "I know that."

That single look was all it took to send her body temperature soaring, and once again she found her gaze playing over him, admiring the sleek, powerful lines of his body. Even dressed casually as he was, in his everyday uniform of a long-sleeved cotton shirt worn with boots and jeans, she found him devastating.

Of course, he did do something to a pair of jeans that was probably illegal in certain states. But then again, he'd look good in anything.

Or nothing, some outrageous little voice supplied.

It was a dangerous thought, prompting images of how he'd looked standing naked at her window on Saturday night, and what it had felt like to run her fingers through the glossy softness of his hair and taste the intoxicating flavor of his mouth.…

"Glory?"

She gave a guilty jerk. "What?"

"Do you want to go or not?"

Was the ocean vast? Was the sky blue? Could he make her hyperventilate with just a look? "I'd love to."

He gave her a decidedly male smile. "Good."

Happiness raced through her, while the hopes for the future she'd been trying to talk herself out of earlier began to seem a little more real.

Feeling almost giddy, she was seized by a sudden burst of mischievousness, and found herself giving Logan's big quarter horse an obvious once-over. "That dun have a name?" she asked blandly, recognizing the gelding as one Josh had pointed out as being his uncle's favorite.

Logan's brows rose slightly. "Top Gun."

"Oh, really?" Her voice held a carefully calculated note of surprise as she collected Je'zhar, who took a few mincing steps, sensing her exhilaration. "Interesting choice. Particularly since he looks like a kid's hobbyhorse could outrun him."

She had to give Logan credit; after only a split second of surprise, his eyes began to gleam at the insult.

But by then, of course, Je'zhar's nose was out and his tail was high and he was well into a full running stride. "Hey, Bradshaw," she hollered over her shoulder. "You look pretty good eating my dust!"

He melted into the saddle and set the dun hurtling after her. "Hey, princess," he replied, his dark voice carrying easily as he began to close the distance between them. "You'd better run—'cuz you sure can't hide."

A chill of excitement shot down her spine. With a hoot of appreciative laughter, she turned around and did as he advised.

Ten

Gloryanne found the slip of paper with the telephone number on it Wednesday morning. Christopher's frog, Brutus, led her to it.

She'd already started to pack the washer with dirty clothes when the previous day's near disaster made her pause. It had been pure luck that Brutus, as Christopher had informed her was the name of the creature she'd retrieved from the pocket of his about-to-be-washed shirt yesterday, had made a fortuitous noise. Otherwise, he'd have been one well-laundered little frog.

Unfortunately, Christopher had a habit of repeating himself, and the chances were that if Brutus was visiting her today, he wouldn't be so accommodating as to announce his presence. And since the last time Glory had checked, frogs weren't classified as wash 'n' wear, it seemed a search was the order of the day.

So with a sigh, she hauled the clothes back out of the washer and rather gingerly checked pockets, but to her relief found nothing but a half-eaten candy bar, a hoof pick—and Anne Bradshaw's name and telephone number, written on a scrap of paper in Josh's distinctive scrawl.

Yet Josh hadn't said a word about calling his mother, she realized uneasily. And when she stopped to think about it, there'd been an undercurrent of strain between him and Logan the past few days. So what exactly, she wondered, staring down at the offending piece of paper, was going on?

She might not know now, but she intended to find out.

She got her chance later that day after Josh's riding lesson. They'd put the horses away and were sitting on the tack room floor, getting ready to clean some equipment, when Glory pulled out the slip and handed it to him. "I found this when I was doing the laundry this morning," she said, not wanting him to think she'd been prying on purpose.

His expression initially curious, he took it from her, only to stiffen when he saw what it was. "Thanks," he said, slipping it into his shirt pocket. And without another word, he resumed dismantling a bridle.

Her uneasiness increasing, Glory picked up one of the reins he'd unfastened, silently noting his uncharacteristic clumsiness as he fumbled with the other buckles, a rather good indicator, she imagined, of his inner distress.

She began working saddle soap into the leather, her own hands deft. "So," she said after a minute, carefully keeping her voice only mildly curious, "did you ever talk to your uncle?"

He paused and glanced up, his expression abruptly wary. "Yeah. For all the good it did me. He clammed up just like he always does."

Remembering Logan's brief responses to her own questions the evening on the ridge, Gloryanne made a sympathetic sound. Still, her feelings for the man she loved made her want to give him the benefit of the doubt—and it didn't sound as though Josh had been too open about *his* feelings, either. Thoughtfully she asked, "Did you tell him how you feel?"

The boy squirmed. "Well…maybe not exactly. I kind of thought I'd work up to it—but before I could, he said all the usual stuff, and well…that was it."

Again, Glory gave Logan the benefit of the doubt. "Maybe there isn't anything more he can tell you. I know it's hard, but you may just have to accept the idea that your mom puts her career ahead of *everything*. She must know how much your uncle loves you, and she may feel the best thing for all of you is to get on with your lives."

"Maybe," he said, vigorously rubbing a sponge across the tin of saddle soap until he had a rich lather, his eyes glued to his hands. "But I don't think so."

There was something in his tone that increased Glory's anxiety. "Why not?"

"Because," he admitted reluctantly. "I called her. And when I asked her why she never came to see us anymore, she started to cry." His put down the sponge, giving up any pretense of business as usual, and turned to Glory with a face filled with pain and confusion.

"Oh, Josh…" She stared at him, her mind whirling with all the possible reasons for Anne Bradshaw's surprising reaction.

"Yeah," he said, his sense of helplessness obvious, "it was really awful. I mean, it was nice to find out that she doesn't hate me and everything, but... It never occurred to me she'd come unglued just because I called. The whole conversation was a bust. She said something I didn't understand about being too proud for her own good, but mostly she just sniffled and kept saying how much it meant to her that I'd called, and that it was a sign, whatever that means."

Surely Logan had had something to say about *that*, Glory thought. She tilted her head to one side. "So what did your uncle say?" She was beginning to feel as if that was all she ever asked.

Josh's shoulders slumped, and the misery on his face increased. "I haven't told him I called her," he confessed.

"You're kidding." Oh, how she hoped he was kidding.

"No. I sort of lost my temper when he got all weird and silent on me, and so I told him I wanted to talk to my mom. I was trying to get a rise out of him, you know? But instead he said I should let it go until we heard from her at Thanksgiving." His blue eyes met hers, pleading for understanding. "But I just couldn't wait that long, Glory."

Glory digested that piece of news. "Well... Then, you'd better talk to him now."

The boy gave an adamant shake of his head. "No."

"But, Josh," she said reasonably. "He's bound to find out."

"I don't see how." He gave her a long look, and the next thing she knew, there was a faint note of suspicion in his voice and the sort of cynical look she usually saw on Logan's face. "Unless you're planning to tell him."

Her stomach knotted. "I'm not going to need to," she said, "because you're going to tell him first."

He shook his head again. "Oh, no, I'm not."

"Oh, yes, you are," she said firmly. "Use your head. He'll find out anyway the minute he gets a look at the phone bill." By the stricken expression on his face, it was obvious he hadn't thought of that. "And what if your mom calls back?"

His eyes widened; apparently that particular possibility had eluded him, too. "All right," he said, sighing despondently, the line of his shoulders getting even lower. "You win. I'll talk to him." He thought for a minute and then added, "But not until after the dance, okay? If he finds out now, he'll probably ground me for going behind his back, and I'd never be able to explain to Jennifer."

She stared at him, her first instinct to insist he find his uncle and tell him right now. But although she doubted that Logan would be so unreasonable that he'd punish Josh by refusing to let the boy go to the dance, she had to admit she was reluctant to put it to a test. Her relationship with Josh had progressed a lot, but if she forced him to admit what he'd done to Logan, or divulged what she knew herself, and Logan did forbid the boy to go the dance, their still-fragile friendship might never recover.

Yet at the same time, the memory of how she'd told Logan on that magical night they'd made love that she didn't have anything to hide was crystal clear in her mind. And here she was, only a handful of days later, contemplating keeping quiet about something that vitally concerned him. And the level of trust in *their* relationship was tentative at best; she wasn't at all sure how he'd view her conflicting loyalties—and she'd prefer not to find out.

"Please, Glory?" Josh begged. "I promise I'll tell him on Sunday. If you don't count today, that's only four days."

"Josh…" She couldn't help but be appalled at the position he was putting her in.

"Please? What difference will it make?"

A lot, said a little voice in her head.

Still, as much as she might wish otherwise, it was impossible not to respond to the blatant plea in his earnest blue eyes. "Okay," she said unhappily. "I think what you're doing is wrong—I think you should tell your uncle now—but I'll respect your right to make your own choice in this. You've got until Sunday noon." It wasn't as if anything cataclysmic was going to happen between now and then, she tried to tell herself.

"All *right,*" he said with a huge sigh of relief.

But it wasn't all right, and she knew it. Still, it was only four days. Could it really make that big a difference?

Yes, warned her little voice, direly predicting that this was going to blow up in her face.

She tried to silence it by reminding herself of Josh's and Chris's conviction that Logan's bark was worse than his bite, and by promising herself that she'd talk to Logan herself right after Josh did on Sunday. Surely he'd understand.

And if he doesn't? the voice persisted.

He would, she told herself, firmly setting aside her misgivings as she picked up her sponge and went back to work.

He had to.

* * *

When Gloryanne opened her door Saturday night, she was wearing a fuzzy, cream-colored sweater dress that rendered Logan momentarily speechless.

It was a deceptively simple garment, with long sleeves and a softly draped neckline, but it was short enough to expose a tantalizing length of pretty legs— and what there was of the rest of it hugged her curves like a lover's embrace.

"Come on in," she said, pushing open the screen. "I need to get my purse. Did the boys get off all right?"

Thankfully, he found his voice. "Yeah. Christopher was all excited about spending the night with the Nielsens, and Josh and his friend and the friend's older brother—the one who's old enough to drive— left just a little while ago to collect their dates."

"I hope he has fun tonight."

"He will," Logan murmured, feeling as if someone had turned up the thermostat as she led the way into the living room and he noticed the seductive slit up one side of her skirt. "Hey, princess," he said huskily, getting a peek of one slim, silk-clad thigh. "You look terrific tonight."

Even as he said it he knew he was understating the case, and when she flushed with pleasure and murmured a flustered "Thanks," he was sure of it. He recalled his first impression of her as being only passably pretty and wondered how he ever could've been so blind.

She was so lovely it made him ache.

Her hair was loose, a smooth curve of pale brown silk threaded with gold; with a mild jolt he discovered that the only other time he could recall seeing it down had been the night that they'd made love....

Just the thought was enough to kick his libido into overdrive and plunge him into a landslide of desire so intense it virtually stole his breath. And for an instant—a very long instant—he was tempted to see if he couldn't talk her into skipping the dance altogether so they could spend the entire evening repeating that pleasurable experience.

She picked her small suede purse up off the table and turned, faltering as she saw the shuttered, heavy-lidded look he was giving her. "Are you all right?" she asked uncertainly.

He glanced down at the cardboard container clutched in his hand, feeling more than a little foolish as he saw that he'd inadvertently crushed one corner. Hell. Here he was, a grown man, and he was acting like some sweaty-palmed teenager.

"Yeah." He thrust the box at her. "Here. This is for you." Seeing her hesitation as she stared at the box in surprise, he felt another one of those disconcerting zaps of juvenile insecurity.

She took it from him and slowly opened it, taking out a delicate spray of flowers fashioned to be worn as a wrist corsage. She was silent for a long moment, her head bent as she looked at the pale pink gardenias before her eyes lifted to his.

The look in those dark, velvet depths made him feel ten-feet tall—until he saw she was also blinking back tears. The desire that had been pounding through him momentarily retreated, replaced by an alarming surge of tenderness. "Hey," he said awkwardly, "it's just a few flowers. It's no big deal—I just thought it might be fun, sort of remind you of your high school years.''

She shook her head, her voice low and husky as she said, ''I never went to any of the dances. I was kind of shy, and I changed schools too often....'' She slipped the floral bracelet on her wrist and reached up to rest her hand against his cheek, immersing him in the flowers' delicate fragrance—and her own intoxicating scent. ''They're perfect, Logan. Thank you.'' She rose up on tiptoe to press a kiss of aching sweetness to his mouth.

His hand sought the warm hollow at the base of her spine, urging her closer, his mind reveling in the perfect fit of her lips against his and the absolute rightness of holding her in his arms as he deepened the kiss.

Need blazed through him.

Her purse dropped to the floor.

Their bodies met, coming together like matching puzzle pieces, the gently rounded curve of her hip and breasts cradling his more angular lines, their breaths mingling, their tongues tangling, their hands gently stroking each other. His mouth was hot and firm and hungry as his lips tasted hers, and Glory couldn't seem to stop touching him, seeking the satiny hardness of him as she molded herself to his length and he began to rock against her. It was an instinctively enticing rhythm, which she answered with a beguiling motion of her own.

Her unconditional surrender threatened the borders of Logan's control. Trying to ignore the relentless surge of his blood that was demanding completion, he struggled with a wildfire urge to carry her down to the floor and satisfy the hunger riding them both.

His heart pounding, his pulse racing, he broke off the kiss while he still had the power to, swallowing a heartfelt groan as he rested his cheek against the top of Glory's silky head and battled to regain his breath.

With a soft little sound of protest, Glory tilted her head, her lips brushing his throat. "Do we have to stop?" she asked shakily, her warm moist breath tickling against him like an invitation.

He made a sound that was partway between a laugh and a groan. "We do if you want to go to the dance."

Her arms tightened around his waist and she began to string a chain of kisses up his neck. "Let's stay home, then," she said breathlessly.

He weighed his desire, which was urging him to leap at her suggestion, against the wistfulness that'd been in her voice when she'd revealed that she'd never been to a dance.

Growing up the way she had, there were probably a lot of things she'd missed out on, he reflected. Compared to some of them, the simple pleasure of a high school dance probably wasn't much.

But it was still the only thing it was within his power to give her, and for reasons that he didn't entirely understand, it was important to him that he see it through.

Stepping back, he brushed the corner of her mouth with a kiss. "Don't tempt me."

"But Logan—"

"No," he said, before he changed his mind. "I want to take you. And besides, things have been a little tense between Josh and me lately, and I don't want to disappoint him." Despite his painfully aroused body, a gleam of amusement sparked to life in his navy eyes, "I'm supposed to help keep this affair on the straight and narrow, remember?"

"I forgot," Glory admitted, feeling a sharp flash of anxiety at his mention of Josh. *Tomorrow,* she consoled herself. *I'll talk to him tomorrow whether Josh does or not.*

She took a calming breath and forced her uneasiness to retreat, her gaze drifting admiringly from her date's nubby gray sports coat to his fashionably pleated black slacks to the dressy black cowboy boots he was wearing. His crisp white shirt turned his skin to bronze, making his blue eyes look bluer and his hair appear even glossier than usual. She reached up to smooth his open collar. "The way you look," she said huskily, "you're more likely to inspire a riot than stop one."

The banked fire in his eyes burned a little brighter at her blatant approval. He leaned over and picked up her purse, holding it out to her. "We'd better go," he growled. "Because if you keep looking at me like that, there's going to be a major uprising right here."

Wisely, she didn't comment, but the hand she extended for the purse trembled.

It was a beautiful night for the forty-minute drive to the Nile County high school. As if to honor the dance in its name, a huge harvest moon blanketed the landscape with a milky light. Yet Glory and Logan hardly spoke, the air between them too charged with sexual tension to allow easy conversation.

By the time they arrived, however, they were both feeling nominally more relaxed, and as the evening unfolded they were able to converse more and more easily, discussing things from the pending sale of the orchard to the pros and cons of Western versus English schooling techniques, between turns of dancing and visiting with the other chaperons.

The gymnasium itself was charming, having been decorated to match the night outside, with a huge yellow paper moon strung up against a midnight-blue backdrop. Hundreds of silver-foil stars had been hung from the rafters.

Glory thought it was beautiful. Almost as beautiful as her date.

"So what do you think?" he asked her. After a brief intermission, the band had come back for the second set, and they were standing at the edge of the dance floor, which was crowded with teenagers who were dancing with the same boundless energy they'd shown all night. "Are you having a good time?"

Her eyes shining, she smiled at him. "It's wonderful." It was true; the other chaperons were friendly, the band was surprisingly good, and even though Logan had been called away once or twice—to intervene when an argument got out of hand, to head off a pair of pranksters bent on adding a little zip to the punch—she was thoroughly enjoying herself.

Of course, the main reason for that was Logan himself; intense, a little quiet, perhaps, but as she'd noted, so handsome, and behind his dangerous facade, so truly good....

The song ended, and Josh appeared out of the crowd. "Hey, Glory. Hey, Uncle 'Gun," he said affably, his face flushed from dancing.

"Hey, yourself," Logan answered. "Where's your date? She finally get smart and find a really nice guy?" Josh had been by earlier to introduce them to Jennifer, a stunning young blonde whose every glance at the boy had been adoring.

Josh rolled his eyes. He was in excellent spirits, his quarrel with his uncle apparently forgotten. "She went to the ladies' loo," he explained irrepressibly, "to do girl things."

Logan and Glory exchanged an amused look.

The teenager shoved his hands in his pockets and tried to look nonchalant. "I was sort of wondering…"

"Yes?" Logan prompted patiently.

"Well… Some of the guys and their dates are going to George for something to eat after the dance." There was an all-night truck stop at the tiny town of George, Washington. "Jason and Eric—" the two brothers with whom he'd come "—called their folks, who said they could go, and I was hoping that it'd be all right with you if I went, too."

Logan looked thoughtful. "When would you be home?"

"Well, see, that's the really good part. I've been invited to spend the night at Jason's, so we wouldn't be out too late because he lives close to George. Just think," a wicked smile tugged at the corners of his mouth as he played what he obviously considered his ace in the hole, "you guys would have the house all to yourselves."

Glory felt her cheeks turn red, while Logan studied Josh. And then, to her even greater embarrassment, the ghost of a smile remarkably similar to his nephew's touched his face. "You're right," he said dryly, the loose drape of his arm tightening fractionally around Glory's slender waist, "that is the good part. So go."

"*Yes!*" Josh gave an enthusiastic punch to the air just as one of the other chaperons, a man who Glory vaguely remembered being introduced to as Bob, tapped Logan on the shoulder.

"Got a minute?" Bob inquired, nodding toward the door where it appeared there were some party crashers from a rival school. After a hurried consultation, the two men excused themselves, heading for the door as the band swung into another song.

Josh took a look around, then tugged on her arm. "Come on. Jen's not back, so you can hang out with me." The song was a moderately slow one so he carefully took her in his arms. "I don't want you to worry," he told her, mistaking the reason for her silence as he stared down at his feet, concentrating on preserving a proper ballroom distance. "I haven't forgotten our deal. I'll be home in the morning to talk to Uncle Logan just like I promised."

It had never occurred to her that he wouldn't, just as it had never occurred to her that the attraction between her and Logan—and their decision to do something about it—was so obvious. "I know you will," she said, responding to his statement while trying to decide how to bring up what was foremost on her mind.

In the end, she simply asked. "Josh? Does it bother you that your uncle and I…that I like him?"

His gaze jerked from his feet to her face. "Heck, no," he said hastily. He smiled, clearly a little uncomfortable with the subject, but compensating well. "It used to worry me, him being so alone, even though I'd like to stick around after graduation and help with the horses, you know? But…the last few weeks have been nice. Christopher and I…we like having you around."

It wasn't exactly an effusive compliment, but it

meant more to Glory than the most fulsome praise. Deeply touched, she impulsively leaned forward and pressed a quick kiss to the boy's cheek. "Thanks. You're a good friend."

A tide of scarlet raced up his neck, but he brazened it out, even managing a creditably devilish smile that was all budding Bradshaw. "Hey, you know, you're not too bad, either—for an older lady."

She fought a smile. "You'd better watch it, or I'll tell all your friends how I dunked you in the pond and beat you to shore. Think what it'd do to your macho image."

He pressed a hand to his heart in mock horror. "Gosh—social ruin! And after everything Uncle 'Gun did to blacken the family name."

She was immediately intrigued. "Like what?"

"The guy's a legend around here," Josh informed her importantly. "He's credited with single-handedly chaining an outhouse to the main doors for three April Fools' Days in a row—without ever getting caught. And they say he dangled a teacher who ticked him off out a second-story window by his heels. I mean, is that cool, or what?"

"Definitely 'or what,'" Logan said, startling them both as he came up behind Glory. He motioned his nephew away with a jerk of his head. "Go find your own date, brat, and quit trying to ruin me with mine. Otherwise, I may change my mind about turning you loose on an unsuspecting countryside."

Grinning, the boy stepped away with alacrity, making a slight but courtly bow as he let his uncle take his place.

"Oh—and Josh?" Logan stopped the boy with a hand to his shoulder as his nephew started to turn away. "Don't do anything dumb, okay? And don't believe everything you hear. There's no way I'd do anything as irresponsible as holding someone out a window by their heels." He paused, then added blandly, "I had a really firm grip on the guy's ankles."

Josh gave a bark of laughter and disappeared.

Logan watched the boy go with a faintly ironic smile before he turned to Glory. "Kids." He shook his head. "I can't figure him out. First we had words Sunday night and he was barely speaking to me, and then the last few days he's been acting like this. Strange."

Guilt instantly raised its ugly head inside her—guilt and a compelling desire to blurt out everything she knew. Yet even as she opened her mouth to speak, a vision of Josh's anguished eyes when he'd confided his conversation with his mother sprang into her mind, and she swallowed the words ready to spill off her lips—wishing it was as easy to curb her regrets. Feeling like the worst sort of hypocrite, she forced herself to say, "How do you mean?"

Logan gave a mirthless smile. "He's been real amenable, like nothing ever happened—which usually means he's hiding something. Don't worry about it. Whatever it is, he'll get around to telling me pretty soon. Secrecy isn't exactly Josh's strong suit."

It wasn't hers, either, Glory knew, anxiety cramping her stomach like a closed fist.

He ran his hand down her arm, an oddly reassuring gesture. "Relax," he said softly. "Whatever it is, Josh and I will work it out. We always do."

They both fell silent, then, lost to their own thoughts as they danced, a subtle swaying motion that was the only movement possible in the crush of other dancers.

It was a while later that Glory lifted her head. "Were you really such a hellion in high school?" she asked, needing a distraction from her worries. She found it hard to reconcile the intense man she knew with the exuberant youngster Josh had described.

"No," he said, but there was a light in his eyes that suddenly made the two images seem less incongruent. "Although I did once mastermind a brilliant prank that involved a few cases of instant pudding and the teachers' washroom." At her startled look, his faint air of devilry increased. "And the entire staff did chip in to buy me a graduation gift."

Completely charmed, she laughed, low and throaty, and he went very still. "God, you look beautiful when you do that," he said, staring down at her.

Startled by his sudden intensity, she looked up to see that his face had gone tight with desire, and the knowledge that he wanted her went through her like a hot knife through butter.

The band launched into a slow, intense torch song.

Wordlessly, he gathered her closer.

Intoxicated by the faintly spicy scent of his aftershave, entranced by the very masculine bunch and shift of his muscles beneath her palms, Glory leaned against him, her body heating from his proximity as well as the feelings surging through her. Closing her eyes, she moved in time to the slow throbbing beat, letting herself get lost in the music and the heaven of being in Logan's arms.

Several minutes later, he said quietly, "Glory?"

"Hmm?"

"Would you mind if we left? Bob said he'd cover for me."

She leaned slightly back to look up at him. "Is something wrong?"

"Yeah." He broke the link of his hands around her waist so he could trace a little circle over the sensitive indentation of her spine. "If we don't leave soon, I'm going to strip you naked and make love to you right here."

She blinked, certain she couldn't have heard him right, yet even so, a vision sprang to mind of the two of them, their bodies intimately intertwined, while all around them the music throbbed and surged, building to a shattering crescendo....

"What did you say?" Her throat was suddenly so tight it was hard to squeeze the words out.

"Let's go home." His hands kneaded gently, sliding even lower on her back.

She shuddered at the passion that turned his voice to smoke, unable to do more than nod her acceptance as she was claimed by a potent need to taste his mouth and feel his bare skin against her own aching flesh, and to know again the soul-stealing power of his possession.

They left without another word, careful not to touch except for the fragile bond of their hands, and although Logan made the drive in record time, it still seemed like a long, long time before they arrived back at the ranch. As if they were no older than the adolescents they'd just left, they shared a series of impassioned kisses as they made their way toward the darkened house and onto the shadowy porch, where Fred, who had yet to show much mettle as a watch-

dog, yawned and thumped his tail in greeting without
ever leaving his bed.

Savoring a sense of rising anticipation, the two of
them slipped into the kitchen where the stove light
shone, a single beacon in the sea of the night. Logan
started for his bedroom.

"Wait." Tugging her hand free of his, Gloryanne
slipped off the gardenia bracelet he'd given her and
crossed to the refrigerator. After one last gentle touch
to a petal, she placed it carefully inside. "There," she
said quietly, her voice a contented whisper threading
the silence. She made her way back to him and took
his hand and together they traversed the short distance
to his room.

He turned the bedside lamp on low and straightened, taking in her softly disheveled hair and the desire tinting her cheeks with rose. His own eyes were
dark with some emotion she couldn't read. "I had a
wonderful time," she said softly.

"Good." He reached down and gently brushed
back a strand of golden brown hair with one long,
lean finger. "But the night's not over yet, princess."
His hand grazed her cheek on its trip to her waist.
And then, as he drew her more securely into his arms,
he lowered his head, kissing her with an intensity that
threatened her sanity even as it filled her heart.

His mouth, warm and male and insistent, plundered
hers, claiming her breath for his own. His hands, big
and insistent, yet surprisingly gentle, shaped her to
him until she could feel every shuddering breath he
drew into his lungs and the growing tension in all of
his satin-over-steel muscles.

Sinking onto the bed, he drew her into the notch
of his thighs and slowly began to ease her dress up

the slim length of her legs, his mouth never leaving hers until they had to come up for air so he could draw the garment over her head.

Easing back, Logan gave her a long, lazy once-over and uttered a low, heartfelt oath as she stood before him in her high heels and he saw what had been hidden beneath the cream-colored angora clutched in his hand. A wisp of a French lace bra the same color as the gardenias he'd given her cradled her breasts, a pair of matching panties followed the curve of her hips, and a lace-encrusted garter belt held up her hose. The dress slipped from his suddenly nerveless fingers.

"God, but you're full of surprises." Dark hair tumbling over his brow, he gave a shaky laugh. "If I'd had any idea that was all you had on under that temptation to sin you were wearing, we never would've made it out of your apartment earlier."

Her dark eyes turned the color of warmed brandy. "Some things are worth waiting for," she advised him, her solemn tone belied by the feverish way her hands were busy with buttons, boots and zipper as she helped him out of his clothes.

When he was down to nothing but a pair of navy briefs, he sat back down on the bed and again drew her close, cupping the fragile line of her jaw in one warm, slightly callused palm. "You're trouble, you know that?"

"I'm trying," she said huskily, her words lost to a sudden gasp as the silky dark tickle of his hair whispered across her breasts when he dipped his head and pressed a kiss to the shallow oval of her navel, his lips trailing unhurriedly upward as he unsnapped her bra and weighed her breasts in his palms. And then his mouth closed over one turgid tip, and she lost her ability to function rationally at all.

His mouth was like silken fire, searing, touching, igniting her ardor as he tasted her, first one breast and then the other, and then the first all over again, until she was a liquid flame of pleasure dancing to the sensuous music pouring from his hands and mouth.

Deftly stripping away the remainder of their clothes, the extent of Logan's need was obvious as he fell back on the bed, watching through eyes that were nearly black as Glory reacted instinctively, fanning the flames between them even higher as she straddled his thighs, pinning his shoulders to the bed with her small hands. Her mouth trailed hungrily across his heaving chest, testing the firm heat of his skin with the petal softness of her lips.

"Glory," he said with a hoarse laugh, protesting his own helplessness as her caresses turned his muscles to jelly.

"Shh," she said, her hair sliding over him like a rustle of silk. She watched with satisfaction when his eyes swept shut at the husky promise in her voice. "Let me love you, Logan. I want to." Even as she trailed kisses from his chest to his mouth, her hips cradled him, guiding him closer.

With a fierce cry of fulfillment, she felt him come sliding home, hard and hot and male inside her, and then she began to move, searching until she instinctively found the motion guaranteed to turn his blood to fire.

"Easy, princess," he gritted out, his hands wrapping gently around her hips as he tried to slow her steadily increasing pace. "Easy..." Her soft little cries were driving him crazy.

"Logan!" She went arching away from him and then flying back, intent on escaping the gentle pressure of his hands, getting lost in the symphony of passion the two of them were creating.

"Dammit, Gloryanne, I wanted to make this last," he gasped, the last scrap of his control disappearing completely as the soft glove of her body grew tighter and tighter, drawing him out of himself and into her. "I wanted to make it good for you, princess, I wanted to feel you go all hot and liquid around me, I wanted to hear you cry out—"

His wish was fulfilled as her mouth silenced him and she went wild in his arms, so that he felt as much as heard her cry of rapture, and then he was filling her, lifting her with him as he exploded upward in a completion that made him feel as if he was shattering into a thousand pieces even while he felt more complete than he ever had before.

For one brief, breathtaking instant they were one heart, one mind, one body meshed together in absolute perfection, and in that diamond-pure moment Logan had a clear picture of what his future could be....

And then the thought was gone, lost in a wave of varying emotions—tenderness, humor, affection— and something fierce and possessive and protective that he couldn't seem to name, as Gloryanne gave him a nip on the ear and collapsed on top of him with a sigh of utter feminine satisfaction.

"You okay?" he asked, his voice slow and deep, his fingers lazily smoothing the satin of her hair before sliding slowly down her back, languidly stroking the sleek velvet of her skin. He frowned slightly at the realization that he couldn't seem to stop touching her.

Smiling, she pressed a kiss to the base of his throat and twined her arms around his neck, and as easy as that she began to drift into sleep. "Never better, cowboy."

He looked down at the dark lashes fanning the smooth surface of her cheek and tipped up her chin, flexing upright so he could brush his lips against her lushly parted pink mouth, smiling a little to himself as she sighed again and snuggled closer.

"I love you," she whispered against his lips.

And in the next instant, she fell fast asleep.

Eleven

Since when, Logan wondered, lying lazily in bed the next morning, had the aroma of coffee become an aphrodisiac?

Since Glory started making it, he answered his own question, not even bothered by the inanity of the mental exchange as he lay listening to the quiet sounds she was making in the kitchen. He tried to identify the emotions rolling through him.

Satiation?

Certainly.

Exhaustion?

Absolutely.

Satisfaction?

Unequivocally.

Happiness?

Just the thought was alarming.

Yet the longer he looked at it, circling and prodding

the effervescent emotion bubbling through him with all the same caution he'd accord a wounded grizzly, the safer it seemed. There didn't seem to be any teeth or claws to this particular beast. As a matter of fact, he felt as if he could take on the world—and he hadn't felt that quixotic in years.

But still... Happiness? When had it happened?

Looking back over the past few weeks, the only thing that seemed clear was that there wasn't a single moment that he could point to and say, *There—that's the one.* No, his newfound contentment sprang from a combination of simple everyday things; a clean shirt, a quiet word, the aroma of a pot roast simmering, laughter warming an early morning—the knowledge that someone else shared his concerns.

He propped his hands behind his head and stared sightlessly at the ceiling, remembering the words Glory had murmured last night before she'd drifted off to sleep.

I love you.... She'd spoken so quietly she'd barely stirred the air, and yet the words had echoed endlessly inside his head.

I love you. Three little words, and he'd had no idea how much it would mean to him to hear her say them.

Or how great the temptation would be to say them back—whether he meant them or not.

He looked up as she slipped through the doorway, a cup of coffee clutched in each of her slender hands. "Good morning." Barefoot and dressed in a pair of jeans and a lemon-colored sweatshirt, with her hair once more caught up in a ponytail, she looked about thirteen.

But it'd been no child in his bed last night. It had been a ripe, full-grown temptress, a creature of silk skin and desire, who'd taken him places he'd never been before and shown him elements of himself he hadn't known existed.

She handed him a mug and perched on the foot of the bed, her expression appreciative as she skimmed his naked chest and rumpled hair with eyes as warm and liquid as melted chocolate. "Hungry?"

His gaze played over her in turn, a bright blue lick of heat. "Yeah—you could say that."

Glory felt a tinge of pink blossom high on her cheeks. She had a vague memory of him rolling out of bed before first light to feed the stock—and a much more vivid one of him returning. He'd slipped back into bed smelling deliciously of horses, hay, and fresh air, kissed her awake, and then proceeded to make love to her with languid power, fanning the embers of her desire until she'd been wild beneath him, crying out with a need only he could satisfy.

She took a sip of coffee. "Aren't you tired?"

"Tired?" One brow rose in muted incredulity. "Of hearing all those soft sounds you make when I'm buried deep inside you?" He sent her a wolfish grin. "Not in this lifetime, princess."

She gave him a long, level look, not wanting to let on how much she treasured his unaccustomed teasing and said primly, "Even so, you'd better get up. I told Bridget I'd pick Christopher up around noon, and Josh should be home by then as well." By the time she got back, Josh would have had a chance to talk to Logan—and then, if he gave her the chance, it would be her turn to explain herself.

He took a quick sip of coffee and glanced at his watch—the only thing he had on. "Maybe, maybe not. He and Jason probably stayed up half the night and talked. We have plenty of time.''

''For what?'' she said, although she had a pretty darn good idea.

Setting his mug on the nightstand, he took hers and did the same. ''For this.'' He reached for her and pulled her beneath him, his mouth settling hungrily over hers.

For the first few minutes he was content just to kiss her, his lips lazily plying hers, his tongue making a series of slow advances and even slower retreats, his strong white teeth gently worrying her bottom lip, then sponging it with kisses.

But it wasn't long before kissing wasn't enough for either of them and his long, clever fingers were sneaking up under the hem of her sweatshirt, mapping the smoothness of her midriff and tickling over her ribs, to settle finally over her lace-covered breasts. Shaping her with his hands, he rubbed her nipples with his thumbs, over and over until they were aching points against his palms.

His mouth slid across the delicate line of her cheek to her ear, his breath tickling deliciously against that ultra-sensitive shell. ''Pardon me, princess, but... don't you think you're a little overdressed?''

Given that he was wearing nothing, which was impossible to overlook given the enthusiastic way the lower part of his body was pressed firmly against her soft, feminine core, she supposed he had a point. Still, she was enjoying his surprising lightness of heart so much that she hated to see it end, even to move on to more...athletic events. Slowly rotating her pelvis against his, she asked innocently, ''Think so?''

''Impudent witch...'' He lowered his head to taste

the laughter on her lips, deftly unsnapped her jeans, and began to peel them down—only to freeze at the sound of an insistent knock at the door, which was quickly joined by Fred's high-pitched yapping.

His face settling into a distinct scowl, Logan rolled reluctantly onto an elbow. "Who the hell can that be?" he muttered with a fierce glare at his wristwatch. "It's barely after ten."

Glory scooted off the bed, trying to tug her sweat-shirt down and her jeans up and smooth her hair all at the same time. "Maybe Josh forgot his key. I'll go see."

Moving more slowly, Logan reluctantly swung his legs to the floor, and was just starting to reach for the clothes when Glory slipped out the door.

By the time she returned, he'd managed to pull on his ancient, disreputable, black denim jeans, although he was still bare-chested. His boots clutched in his hand, he took one look at her ashen face and his own paled considerably. "Which one is it?" he said tersely.

It took her a second to understand that he thought something had happened to one of the boys. "Oh, Logan, no," she quickly reassured him. "It's not about either of the kids. It's a woman, asking for you. She's waiting in the kitchen."

For a moment he just stood there. Then he set his boots down and stomped into them, taking a moment to collect himself as he tugged his pant legs over the tops. When he straightened a heartbeat later, a vee of curiosity had formed between his brows. "So why are you looking at me like that?"

Bending over to pick up his shirt, she realized her suspicion regarding the woman's identity must be showing on her face. Never any good at dissembling, she said honestly, "Because I think maybe's it's Josh's mom." She drew his chambray work shirt through her hands, oddly comforted by the motion.

"Did she tell you that?" he asked.

"No, but—"

"Then forget it. There's about a snowball's chance in hell of my sister showing up here uninvited." He took the shirt out of her hands and shrugged into it. "Trust me. It's probably just some woman interested in a horse. People drop by unexpectedly all the time. Although—" he shot a regretful look at the bed before he headed out the door "—whoever this is, she sure has a lot of nerve showing up at this hour on Sunday morning."

"Logan—" But he was gone before she could stop him, silencing Fred with one firmly worded command as he strode out of the room. Glory followed helplessly in his wake, praying that he was correct and that the woman was really only someone who'd been passing by. But she didn't think so.

She was right. Logan took one look at their early morning caller and stopped, the rigid line of his back indicating that the woman was no stranger. All at once feeling inexplicably like an intruder, Glory moved off to one side, her breath catching in her throat as she got a look at the animosity transforming his features.

"Well, hell." Gone was the playful lover of a few minutes earlier. In his place was a hard-faced man with a frighteningly implacable look in his eyes. "You always did have lousy timing, sis. Six damn years—more than three hundred lousy weekends—and you have to pick this one to show up."

"It's nice to see you, too, 'Gun." Outwardly, at least, Anne Bradshaw appeared unperturbed by her brother's less-than-gracious welcome. She was a tall, slim woman with a short cap of medium brown hair salon-streaked with blond, and although she didn't look much like Logan, they did share the same dark blue eyes and a look of wary distrust that no one could mistake.

Yet for a second, Glory would've sworn she saw a glimmer of naked yearning on both their faces, although it was gone before she could be certain.

"So how have you been?" Anne continued in that same polite tone.

"Oh, just great." Logan's response was like a rifle shot; short, succinct—and deadly.

As if her absence had been one of days instead of years, Annie set her purse on the table and walked unhurriedly over to the cupboard, with the kind of unconscious confidence that came from having grown up in a place. Opening a cabinet door and taking down a mug, she poured herself a cup of coffee, and Gloryanne suddenly found herself cast back to her childhood and the many times she'd felt as she did now—an outsider looking in.

"I'm sorry it's so early." Cup in hand, Anne turned to stand with her back against the counter. "But I took a red-eye flight from the Capitol and drove straight through from Seattle." Dressed in pristine beige linen slacks and a fashionable blue silk blouse, she looked rested and energetic, not at all like a woman who'd spent half the night on an airplane.

Logan brushed impatiently past her attempt at small talk, his eyes touching pointedly on her elegant hands with their perfectly manicured nails. "Why didn't you call? Obviously you didn't break all ten fingers—which is about the only excuse I'd consider.''

She stiffened. ''I did call, several times yesterday evening. It's hardly my fault that nobody answered. Perhaps you ought to consider joining the twentieth century—surely they have answering machines, Logan, even way out here.''

He didn't deign to respond. ''What are you doing here?''

Annie hesitated, slanting a quick, apologetic look at Gloryanne before again focusing on her brother. ''I'd prefer to talk in private. This is family business, after all.''

Despite the fact that Annie's words weren't meant unkindly, they struck Gloryanne like a blow, reminding her of her status as an interloper. Suddenly self-conscious of her bare feet and baggy sweatshirt, she flushed as she realized what sort of conclusion Anne Bradshaw must've drawn about the nature of her relationship with Logan, and she straightened abruptly away from the wall. ''You're right,'' she said quietly, ''so if you'll excuse me? I do have things to do, and—''

''Wait one damn minute,'' Logan interrupted, his eyes locking on her like a tractor beam, freezing her in her tracks. ''This is my house—and as far as I'm concerned, you've got a heck of a lot more right to be here than she does.''

He turned back to his sister, and although his words were polite, his tone held a distinct warning. ''This is my partner, Gloryanne Rossiter. In addition to being one hell of a hand with the horses, she's been running the house and helping take care of both our sons, and

I can't think of anything you have to say, Annie, that she shouldn't hear.''

Gloryanne had already started to take a step toward the door when his extraordinary declaration made her stop. Startled, her gaze shot to him, but before she could decide whether he really meant what he said or if his words had been prompted by a desire to oppose his sister's wishes, he turned back to Annie and said coolly, ''Now. Why are you here, and what do you want?''

''Josh called me.''

He froze. ''When?''

''On Tuesday.'' Annie sipped daintily at her coffee, noting his surprise over the edge of the mug. ''I take it you didn't know?''

''No.'' He glanced briefly at Glory, then jerked his eyes back to his sister, the line of his mouth turning briefly grim before his face settled once more into a blank mask and he gave a dismissive shrug. ''Still, I can't imagine what he said that was so compelling you decided to come for a visit after all these years.''

Setting her coffee mug down on the counter with a snap, Anne crossed her arms over her chest. ''I came to apologize,'' she said defensively, ''for how badly I've behaved—and to tell you I want to be a part of Josh's life again.''

''Oh, really?'' Walking in her direction, Logan snatched a cup from the cupboard and splashed coffee in its general direction before slapping the glass pot back down so hard it was a miracle it didn't shatter. ''For how long?''

Annie's calm facade crumbled a little. ''For good, dammit!'' She dredged in a deep breath, visibly trying to calm herself. ''Look,'' she said, striving to sound reasonable, "I'm planning on getting married next month, and David and I plan to have a baby."

"Well, at least you're finally getting things in the right order," Logan murmured. "Congratulations."

"Thank you!" she snapped. "I love David—and I'm darned lucky to have found him. But the point is, Logan, I was afraid to tell him about Josh. I messed up this part of my life so much, running away, letting both you and Josh down, that I didn't want to face it. It was easier just to pretend that you didn't exist. But when Josh called...I knew I needed to get things straightened out, that I couldn't start my new family unless I'd made peace with the old one. And when I finally screwed up the courage to tell David about my past, he agreed."

"Yeah?" Logan knew he was being obdurate, but he couldn't seem to help it. She was leading up to something—he knew his sister well—and every instinct he had was screaming that he wasn't going to like it. "Well, that's a real nice sentiment—except that you're about a dozen years late. You've been in Washington, D.C., too long, Annie. Kids aren't like one of your political issues. You can't put them off until it suits your agenda—they have this disturbing habit of growing up."

"Dammit 'Gun, I know that! But all I'm asking for is a chance! Or are you still mad because the last time I was here I criticized you—and made that offer to help?"

He stared at her in disbelief. "You call threatening to take Josh away from me *help?*"

"Yes! No! I don't know! You'd just been divorced and you had Christopher to take care of—and you made me feel so darned useless and guilty, going off and leaving you alone to cope. It seemed like the thing to do!''

"He wasn't a bag of groceries to be passed around, dammit!''

"I know that—now! I made a mistake! But people change—I've changed. I'm ready to be a parent to Josh now.''

"And?'' he prompted knowingly. "Cut to the chase, Annie.''

She took a deep breath and squared her shoulders, looking at him defiantly. "All right, if you want it straight—I'd like Josh to come spend some time with me in Washington, maybe live with David and me for part of the year.''

He stared at her, then shook his head, as if unable to believe what he was hearing. "No,'' he said flatly.

"But, Logan, think of all the advantages I can give him. Private schools, a house with a swimming pool—''

"No—and that's final.''

"Are either of you going to ask me what *I* want to do?''

The question, uttered from just inside the back door, brought the exchange in the kitchen to a halt as both Logan and Annie whipped around to face Josh, whose arrival had gone unnoticed. The boy was staring at the two of them, a kaleidoscope of emotions from surprise to amazement to anger ranging across his face. He let the screen door slam shut as he walked further into the room.

"Josh…'' Transfixed, Annie stared at the son who'd been a little boy the last time she'd seen him, and who was now taller than she was. "Oh, Josh— you're all grown up.''

His gaze shifted from his uncle to her and back again. "Well?" he demanded of Logan. "Are you going to ask me what I want?"

Hearing the challenge in the boy's tone, it was as if Logan reached some sort of decision. His expression closed, he strode past Josh, plucked his hat from the peg next to the door, and jammed it on his head. "Nope."

"Hey, wait a minute!" Josh protested, following after him. "Where are you going?"

Logan turned, his hand on the door. "I've got work to do."

"But we have to talk about this!"

Logan shrugged. "There's nothing to discuss. I've already made my decision." He pulled open the screen.

"Well, it may not be the same as mine!" Josh warned, his voice rising shrilly.

Logan turned back and gave him a brief nod, his eyes unreadable under the shadow cast by his hat. "Yeah, you're right. And there's nothing I can do about it."

And as Josh watched in outraged disbelief, Logan whistled sharply for Fred, and strode away with the puppy gamboling at his heels.

Hurling a lurid curse at his back, Josh spun around and slammed his fist into the wall. "Damn him!" he sputtered, clutching his hand to his chest. Turning to his mother, he said wildly, "When do you want to leave?"

"Why, I d-don't know," Annie stuttered, obviously not prepared for the last few minutes' surprising turn of events. "I mean, I wasn't planning on your coming to live with me right *now*. But I guess... I suppose I could manage—''

"No." For the first time, Glory spoke, her voice low but strong, a pool of calm in what had become a sea of tumultuous emotions.

Josh turned on her. "Why not?" he demanded. Despite his defiant tone, he was looking at her as if she were the only source of light in a very dark tunnel.

"I'm not saying you shouldn't go—'' *Even though it will break Logan's heart, and mine too, if you do.* "But I want you to think about what you're doing. Don't go because you're mad at your uncle and you want to show him up.''

The boy stiffened. "He's the one who walked out! He doesn't care. He just wants his own way!''

"You know better than that.'' Her brisk tone was like a bucket of cold water, forcing him to think.

"Then why did he just take off?''

"He's scared, Josh,'' Glory said gently. All the pieces had come together in her mind as she'd listened to Logan and Annie argue, and she'd seen what apparently neither his sister nor his nephew had; the killing despair darkening Logan's eyes at the thought of one more loss. "If you're old enough to make this decision, then you're old enough to understand. He loves you. He's done everything he could to be your family, and now he's afraid that just because your mother's shown up, you're going to throw it all away.''

"But that's crazy!'' the boy protested. "I wouldn't do that. I couldn't.'' He hesitated, the last of the defiance draining out of him as for the first time he really considered Logan as a human being with strengths and weaknesses, hopes and fears, of his own. "I love him," Josh said suddenly. "Doesn't he know that?"

"Yes." Glory's eyes sought Annie's. "But too many people have said the same thing—and then hurt him, anyway."

There was a pregnant silence, and then Anne Bradshaw sighed and suddenly dropped her eyes under Glory's silent censure. Moving to the kitchen table, she sank onto one of the chairs. "She's right, Josh. First it was your grandmother. Logan was only four when she died, but for months afterward Daddy and I would find him wandering around the house, crying and searching for her. And then later, there was Dad himself, and then me, and finally Melanie. And then the last time I was here, after everything he'd done for me, I threatened to take you away from him, and it was as if it was the last straw, as if right then and there he made a decision to quit taking chances on people."

She sighed again, and sent her son a sad smile. "And I guess, as long as I'm being honest, I might as well admit that I'm really not ready to be a full-time mother, either. I'm just starting to get my life together, and in a few weeks I'm going to have a husband to consider."

She hesitated, her gaze pleading with him to understand. "But I really do want to get to know you, Josh. That is, if you want to, and we can work something out with your uncle. Perhaps we could start with a visit or two, me here, and then you there, and see how it goes?"

Josh sat down, and regarded his mother from across the table. "Well...maybe." And then, incredibly, a crooked little smile tugged at the corners of his mouth. "Actually," he confided, scooting the chair back and balancing it on its two back legs, "the thought of living in Washington, D.C., gives me the creeps. All that pavement and those buildings…" He cocked his head. "Don't you get claustrophobic?"

Suddenly knowing that everything was going to be all right, Glory didn't wait to hear any more. Instead, she slipped quietly out the door, grabbed her tennis shoes from the porch, and went to find Logan.

He was in the barn, cleaning stalls with a feverish energy and a black scowl that spoke volumes about the state of his temper, and he didn't say a word when he looked up and finally saw her.

"Hi," she said anyway, standing well out of his way as he hefted a huge load of dirty straw and tossed it effortlessly into the wheelbarrow. He'd stripped to the waist, and in place of his hat had tied a bandanna around his forehead to keep the hair out of his eyes. Even in the dim light of the barn she could see that the powerful muscles in his arms and back were damp from exertion; they gleamed like oiled bronze.

Her heart contracted as she registered the tension pulling the flesh tight across his cheekbones, and she started to tell him that things were going to work out. But before she had the chance, he spoke first. "Well? Is he packing?" His voice was impassive.

"Oh, Logan, no! Josh isn't going anywhere. Once he got over being angry, he realized that this is where he belongs. And so did your sister."

For a split second he went still, but he recovered almost immediately and resumed shoveling with that same tireless ease.

Puzzled, Glory watched him. "When I left, they

were discussing the possibility of visiting. That is, if it's okay with you.''

"Why not?" Avoiding her curious gaze, he gave a last look around the clean stall, then went out to the storage locker, where he picked up a hundred-pound bale of straw as if it weighed nothing and carried it back across the corridor and into the stall.

Glory's anxiety increased.

"Logan…" She watched as he searched fruitlessly through his pockets for a knife with which to cut the baling twine, his mounting frustration obvious and out of all proportion to the task. "Logan, what's wrong?"

With that, he stopped and finally looked at her—and she flinched at the raw emotion on his face. But still, his voice remained detached. "You knew, didn't you?"

"Knew what?" she asked cautiously.

"That Josh called my sister."

Her heart collided with her knees, but it didn't occur to her to lie. "Yes."

He gave a curt nod. "Yeah, I thought so. Up at the house earlier, it was written all over your face. How long?"

"How long what?" His lack of emotion was starting to truly frighten her.

"How long have you known?"

"Since Wednesday. Wednesday afternoon."

"And you didn't tell me." It wasn't a question.

The reasoned explanation she'd been rehearsing for half a week died on her lips; one look at his face told her that for the moment nothing she said would help. "No."

"No? All you can say is *no*?" Gone was his indifference, and with it the last of his restraint, as all the anguish and frustration he'd managed to suppress through the scene with his sister rocketed to the surface. "Well, sorry, princess but *no* just doesn't cut it!"

As dangerous in the small space as a caged tiger, he whirled and began to pace. "All this time I was afraid I'd start to care for you and you'd take off, but that was never the danger, was it?" The words spilled from him, fast and fiercely.

"Logan, if you'd just listen—"

"No! All the time I was worrying, it was about the wrong damn thing! Everything you've done—the lessons for Josh, the jokes for Chris, the smiles and kisses for me—they weren't because you cared about us! It was all to secure yourself a place!"

"That's not true—"

"Don't give me that! And to think I was actually starting to trust in you!"

"Logan, please," she begged, her eyes huge and dark as she pleaded with him to understand. "Josh confided in me, yes, but I never meant to take anything away from you. I tried to give him the space to do the right thing. I'm sorry! I didn't know what else to do."

"Sorry!" He snatched up the word and hurled it back at her. "You can hang all the pretty excuses you want on it, lady, but the bottom line is that all the time I was thinking how straight you were, you were playing me for a fool!"

"That's not so!" Even as the first tear trickled down Glory's face, her patience snapped. "Would you just listen to me! Yes, I want a place here, but not at your expense! I want a place *with* you. I love you, Logan. You and Christopher and Josh are like the family I never had—''

"Oh, yeah?" he cried harshly, a strong man lashing out at his own unaccustomed sense of uncertainty. "That's where you're wrong! We may be a family— but we're not *your* family. So why don't you quit interfering in things that are none of your damn business?"

Her face drained of color; she took a stumbling step back.

And suddenly, Logan realized what he'd said.

"Dammit!" He felt like he'd been gut-punched when he saw the desolation invade her eyes in the instant before her expression, always so open to him in the past, went blank.

He gave a cry of frustrated self-disgust and, moving with incredible speed, snatched up the entire bale of straw and pitched it violently against the wall, where it exploded into a million pieces.

Straw rained down.

The stall slowly filled with an impressive silence.

Logan dropped his head into his hands, unable to face the emptiness on Glory's face, damning his own heedless tongue as he pressed the heels of his palms to his suddenly aching eyes.

And he knew that everything he'd just accused her of was a lie.

The truth was that he was afraid. Because if he couldn't handle even the threat of losing Josh, how would he ever survive if Glory chose to say goodbye? And yet, how much worse would it be to know that he'd had a chance of happiness, and cravenly thrown it away?

Out of nowhere, he seemed to hear Christopher's voice.

Glory? If something happened to Daddy, would you take care of me?

Everything inside him seemed to still as he heard again the calm certainty of Glory's reply. Not with his head this time, but with his heart.

Yes, Christopher, I believe I would.

And he knew then that if he could only hold her in his arms, everything else would be all right.

And so it was that he dropped his hands to reach for her—

Only to discover that she was gone.

Twelve

"**I**'m telling you," Glory said to Fred, trying to ignore the tears running down her face as she tugged fruitlessly on the lug wrench, "if women ran the world, everyone would be better off. Think about it. No more wars, a balanced budget…Monday Night Ballet."

She paused to scrub the back of her wrist across her swollen eyes, then glanced over at the puppy, who was watching her from the front passenger seat, his muzzle propped mournfully on the window frame. "What do you think?"

He expressed his opinion with an enormous yawn.

So what did she expect from someone named Fred? she wondered, suppressing a little sob. She took an even firmer grip on the wrench, determined to get the bolt unscrewed, since it was the only one still holding her pancake-flat right front tire to the Cherokee. Giving it everything she had, she twisted.

It didn't budge so much as a fraction of an inch.

She straightened, said something succinct regarding the bolt's probable ancestry, and told herself firmly that she wasn't going to give in to the impulse to lay her head down in her hands and howl, which was what she desperately wanted to do.

Instead she gave the lug wrench a vigorous thwack with her foot, and pondered the fix she was in, stuck in the middle of nowhere, on some cow path that probably wasn't even on the map, with a Jeep she couldn't drive and nothing but a male chauvinist dog for company.

It really wasn't her fault, she consoled herself. Who could have predicted she'd have a flat? Or that this one little bolt would prove to be tighter than all of Fort Knox's security? Or that Logan would suddenly turn on her?

We may be a family—but we're not your family.

She flinched, not quite ready yet to think about that.

It was because she'd wanted to put some actual physical distance between herself and those terrible words—and the dreadful hurt they'd caused her—that she'd taken off. It certainly had nothing to do with that disturbing sensation of being an outsider that she'd experienced earlier in the kitchen. And even if she had been feeling a tad oversensitive when she'd gone looking for Logan, that didn't excuse his attack.

But, then, she also hadn't planned on getting lost. In the back of her mind had been some vague notion of driving randomly around, sorting out her feelings and trying to decide what to do about them, until it

was time to go get Christopher. And then the tire had
gone *k-boom.*

She gave the wrench another kick. Only this time
she missed and slammed her tennis-shoe-clad toes
against the unyielding metal of the wheel rim instead.

It hurt like the very dickens. With a muffled oath,
she grabbed her foot and collapsed in a heap on the
ground, finally giving vent to the misery radiating
through her. Like a monsoon, the tears splashed down
in a torrent that went on and on, until she eventually
began to feel curiously hollow.

When the last tear was inevitably spent and all she
could do was shiver and make pathetic little hiccuping
sounds, she wiped her nose on the front of her sweatshirt, too distracted to care when she left a broad
smear of dirt on her cheek, and lay back down on the
ground. Feeling completely drained, she stared
blankly up at the sky and watched the clouds blow
by, until the long night of Logan's loving and the
morning of emotional turmoil snuck up and whisked
her off to sleep.

She'd didn't awake until well in to the afternoon.
Fred had jumped out the window and was lying beside her, snoring in her ear, and although she was stiff
and sore from being too long on the rocky ground,
her mind was remarkably clear.

And this time when she heard Logan's voice in her
head, saying *We're not* your *family,* she found herself
retorting, *Based on what?*

If family was loving people to distraction, wanting
only what was best for them, glorying in their tri-
umphs and sharing in their hurts, then she qualified;
she felt all those things for Logan and the boys.

And if it was a matter of caring, of making sure

you didn't wash a frog or of telling terrible jokes to make a little boy laugh, or saying to a teenager a hundred times, "Keep your heels down and your back relaxed," while you let him learn to ride on the stallion you prized more than your life, then she was entitled to be counted, as well.

And if it was loving a man so much you couldn't stand the thought of him resting his feet on a cold wooden floor, and if you'd do his work as well as your own if it provided him with a much needed rest, and if you'd forgive him anything, *anything*—even some really awful thing he said to drive you away because you'd seen him at his most vulnerable—then she was definitely eligible.

And no big stubborn rancher was going to tell her otherwise.

But how in the heck was she going to set him straight when she was stranded way out here?

She clambered to her feet. There was nothing for it; she'd have to walk. After all, if she stayed here, it might be days before someone found her, and she had a few choice things to say to Logan Bradshaw that simply wouldn't wait.

And besides, she thought as she flung open the Jeep door and prudently shoved her purse under the front seat before locking up the vehicle, how far could it be? Five or six miles? She'd be home in time for dinner.

And so, with Fred at her side, a gleam in her eye, and the spring restored to her stride, Gloryanne set out for home.

Where in the hell was she?

Logan stood in the yard and checked his watch for

what had to be the hundredth time in half that many minutes.

Four-thirty. She'd been gone for more than five hours. Even now, the light was starting to fade, and in another hour it would be gone.

Just like Glory.

By force of will, he stilled the panic rioting inside him. It was ironic, really. For weeks he'd stubbornly predicted that she would leave, and now that she actually had, he was just as stubbornly refusing to believe that she wasn't coming back.

It had taken the shock of his own cruelty for him to realize that of anyone he'd ever known, Gloryanne could be trusted to do exactly what she said. She'd demonstrated that her very first day at Columbia Creek when she'd agreed to take on the cooking and cleaning, and she'd never faltered, not even that night in her apartment when they would have made love—except for her refusal to make a promise she couldn't keep.

She was the most honorable, forthright person he knew.

And he'd paid her back with untold cruelty, saying the one thing guaranteed to crush her tender heart. *We're not your family...so why don't you quit interfering?*

Every time he remembered the look on her face, he felt shamed to his very soul, yet even so he continued to cling tenaciously to the notion that she was going to come home.

Because this *was* her home. And he and Christopher and Josh *were* her family, bound to her by her generous applications of patience and love and laughter. The evidence was everywhere—from the garden taking shape by the back door, to the flowers abloom in his bedroom, from Christopher's artwork carefully taped to the refrigerator door, to the books on English riding stacked in Josh's room. Even the barn wasn't sacrosanct, since that damn stallion set up a racket every time anyone walked through the door, eager to see his Glory.

Logan knew just how he felt.

"Uncle Logan!" The screen door twanged open, and Josh catapulted down the steps, Christopher at his heels.

Despite his agitation, Logan's heart swelled as he watched the two of them come racing toward him, Christopher so fair and small and Josh so dark, so tall—and growing up so quickly.

He and Josh had talked at length earlier. The boy had arrived at the barn on the heels of Glory's departure, and there'd been no way Logan could put off the long overdue discussion that had followed. Josh had finally opened up, pouring out his secret fears and deep-set hurt about the circumstances of his birth, and Logan had been able to listen at last, to offer insight where he could and comfort where he couldn't.

It had been a long and emotional meeting, and things had barely started to level off when Annie had shown up and the three of them had talked some more. Annie had agreed to bring her new husband for Thanksgiving, and although they still had a long way to go, even now Logan's sister was up at the house taking a nap. Logan felt optimistic that they'd finally taken a step toward bridging the gap that had kept them apart for so long.

But by the time *that* talk had started to wind down, the Nielsens had shown up with Chris, which was when Logan had first realized that Glory was gone. And by then, of course, so much time had elapsed that he'd been afraid to go looking for her for fear he'd miss her when she came back.

And so he waited. Maybe it was foolish. Maybe she was gone for good, and he'd get a phone call in a few days telling him where to send the horses and her belongings. But he didn't think so. He refused to think so. Because somewhere along the way she'd resurrected his hope—and now it refused to go away.

"Uncle Logan, listen!" Josh said, while Christopher jumped up and down. "Mac Witke called. He was out riding around on his dirt bike and he found Glory's Jeep!"

Logan died a little as the image of a catastrophic car accident flashed through his head. He squeezed his eyes shut, willing himself to calm down, but even so he nearly didn't register the next part of what Josh said.

"Up on the old Cowlitz service road, a little ways past Pointed Rock, fifteen miles due west of here. Mac said the Jeep had a flat tire, and it looked like she'd tried to change it, and it was the darnedest thing, but—but…"

Logan's eyes flashed open. "What!"

Josh swallowed, clearly reluctant to tell him the next part. "He said that she was…gone. That there was no sign of her, that she'd just…disappeared."

"Wow!" Christopher said, his eyes as big as saucers. "Aliens!"

But Logan wasn't listening. He was too busy telling Josh to fill a canteen and get the flashlight and his bedroll, and then he was running toward the barn.

Because he didn't believe in creatures from outer

space; what he believed in was one small, stubborn woman who was just brave enough—and steadfast and trustworthy and foolish enough—to do whatever it took to keep her word to him and make her way back home.

Someone had moved the ranch.

As improbable as it seemed, it was the only possible answer. Glory had been walking for hours, and as far as she was concerned, if Columbia Creek was where it was supposed to be, she would have been there by now. She was thirsty and tired, her feet hurt, and to add insult to injury, Fred had given out after the first half hour, and was now a deadweight draped across her shoulders like some kind of an odd-dog stole.

All in all, she'd had better days.

She was so sunk in misery that as she trudged up another of the rises that decorated the landscape like bumps on a herd of camels, she almost slammed right into the horse and rider poised on top of the knoll.

"Hey, princess." Seated on his leggy dun, Logan was wearing an indigo shirt, a day's worth of beard, jeans so old they were nearly white, and a big black cowboy hat; he looked like an escapee from the cast of *Desperado*, and Glory had never seen anyone who looked even half so wonderful.

"Logan!"

His eyes were twin slices of jewel-blue. "Want a lift?"

From somewhere her body found enough moisture to glaze her vision with tears at the offer, until she remembered the way they'd parted—and why. With all the dignity she could muster, she straightened her spine. ''No. I'm doing fine, thank you.''

And then she raised her chin and marched right past him.

Logan's first impulse was to lean over, grab her, and haul her into his arms. She was just so damn beautiful—even if her hair was a little wild, and her face was streaked with grime and her clothes looked as though she'd been rolling around in the dirt—and he wanted desperately to touch her and assure himself that she was real.

But there was something very vulnerable about the set of her mouth, something that hinted she was walking a very fine emotional line, and that it wouldn't take much to push her over the edge.

I did that, he castigated himself. It was a painful admission, but it only strengthened his determination to spend the rest of his life making it up to her—if she'd only give him the chance.

He nudged Top Gun, sending the dun ambling after her, and scowled at Fred who was grinning at him from over her shoulder. ''What happened to the dog?'' he inquired.

For a minute he didn't think she would answer. But after a second she said stiffly, ''Nothing. He's just a little tired.''

He's not the only one, Logan thought, gritting his teeth as she stumbled over a rock. ''Sure you don't want to ride?''

A tremor went through her shoulders. ''No.''

Silently, he cursed, and tried to think of a way to convince her that would allow her to give in gracefully. ''I'd watch those rocks if I were you. It's getting close to the end of the season, and only the big-gest, meanest rattlesnakes are still hanging around.''

She stopped as if she'd hit a wall. Very carefully peeling the puppy off her chest, she set him on the ground, then turned, her hands on her hips. ''Very cute, Bradshaw.'' Her lower lip trembled; she got it under control. ''But you didn't drive me away with your awful kitchen, or your crazy rat stew accusation, or even with all your insults about my dog—so if you think some silly rattlesnake story is going to scare me off, you're wrong.''

That did it. Quicker than she could blink, he leaned over and lifted her up across his lap, trapping her between the wall of his chest and the pommel of the saddle. And then, because he couldn't help himself, he wrapped his arms around her and hugged her, glo-rying in the way she fit against him while he thanked God for helping him find her.

Glory sat rigidly within his arms. ''What do you think you're doing?''

He buried his head in the curve of her neck and drew in a deep, shuddering breath. ''You know that place you said you wanted?''

Glory went very still.

He took her hand and touched it to his heart. ''It's right here—if you still want it.''

For a second she simply stared at him, and then she was filled by a burst of joy that lit her up like a floodlight switching on. ''Oh, Logan.'' Her arms went around his neck, one hand stroking gently down his big, hard back. ''Oh, *yes*.''

He raised his head and looked down at her, and everything he felt for her—love and joy and hope for the future—was there to see on his face. He cleared his throat. "I'm sorry for what I said—"

"Shh." She pressed a finger to his lips. "I understand." And incredibly, she did.

His arms tightened around her. "I love you, Glory."

"I love you, too, cowboy," she said softly. And she cupped his face in her hands and tugged him closer to share a long and tender kiss, knowing that she would treasure this man—and cherish this moment—every day for the rest of her life.

The constellations were just beginning their nightly waltz when Glory and Logan rode into the yard at Columbia Creek.

From the barn came the faint sound of Je'zhar trumpeting a welcome, while up at the house every light blazed on and the boys came tumbling out of the door. Glory gave a shiver of happiness.

Logan gathered her closer. "Cold?"

"No. I feel warm enough to heat the entire world."

"Good."

"Except—" He stiffened, and she said quickly, "I'm sorry I didn't tell you about Josh."

The tension left his big body as quickly as it had come. "Well...I suppose I could let you make it up to me."

She was instantly suspicious of the satisfaction she could hear in his voice. "How?"

"Hey, this *is* a conservative community. I guess you'll have to marry me."

"Oh. Well. If you insist..."

His big warm hand wrapped around her smaller one, and he raised it for a kiss. "I do."

Leaning against him, Glory could feel the solid

strength of his big body—and the slow, steady beat of his heart. She sighed with contentment, then turned her head to press a kiss to the slash in his cheek, prompting the boys to begin to whoop and holler, while Fred began to bark.

Beneath her lips, Logan's face creased in a smile. And then he tipped his head and settled his mouth more firmly over hers—and Glory knew she was finally home.

*   *   *   *   *

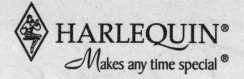

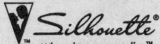

Where love comes alive™

SILHOUETTE *Romance*™

From first love to forever, these love stories are
for today's woman with traditional values.

Silhouette® Desire

A highly passionate, emotionally powerful
and always provocative read.

Silhouette®

SPECIAL EDITION™

Emotional, compelling stories that capture the
intensity of living, loving and creating a family in
today's world.

Silhouette®

INTIMATE MOMENTS™

A roller-coaster read that delivers romantic thrills
in a world of suspense, adventure and more.